Prisms of My Life

MAUREEN YOUNGER

MY Comedy Limited

Maureen's writing is just like her. Direct, insightful, warm but best of all, very very funny.

Jen Brister

The writing is so beautiful it makes you want to be a part of it, more than just a 'reader'.

Ian Moore

Maureen's writing is sharp, incisive, funny and very well observed. Her unique take on life and people is a no holds barred commentary that is colourful, and distinctive just like her stand up. The characters are always memorable, and the stories fascinating.

Shazia Mirza

As funny as I'd expect Maureen Younger's short stories to be, they are also honest, thoughtful and poignant.

VG Lee

DEDICATION

To Dad, thanks so much for everything you've done for me.

To SLO man with heartfelt gratitude for being such a positive influence in my life.

ACKNOWLEDGMENTS

Thanks to all the usual suspects for their unstinting support and for bearing with me despite all my #bemoremaureen moments. Alois, Chris, Christian, Darren, Franz, Ira, Klara, Jen, Jenny, Jayne, Mascha, Micky, Sally, Steph, VG Lee and Walter. Finally, of course, special thanks to everyone I only remembered once I sent this book to print and it was too late to include them.

The Spaniard

Two months left of this shitty job. Two months before she could escape Majorca and her life as a tourist rep. Em hated the job. She hated her life. She hated being exploited and she felt that was exactly what was happening. She wanted to go home. Every evening she would work out in fractions how long she had left. She had roughly one third of her contract to go and then she would be a free woman.

Things were so bad Em had stopped eating properly. It wasn't a conscious decision on her part, but she had never been so thin in her life. The skirt she wore as part of her daily uniform was beginning to swirl around her waist whenever she moved. It was a throwaway comment by the Head Rep, Sharon, that had alerted Em to the fact she might have an eating problem. At first, Em had dismissed the suggestion. It wasn't as if she was on a diet or anything. Em never worried about her figure. She could eat whatever she liked. She'd always been naturally thin.

A few days later during a one-off event organised for all the resort guides, Em was faced with tangible proof that something was wrong. In addition to the live band, the spectacular sea views and the obligatory pep talk, a buffet was the order of the day. Naturally greedy, Em was one of the first to rush to the table and pile a load of food onto her tray. Stumbling under its weight, she sat down and surveyed all the goodies she had grabbed. As she stared at her spoils, it dawned on her she didn't fancy eating any of it. As the lesser of all evils on her tray, she picked up a pot of yoghurt, forced the yoghurt down her throat and already felt full. The thought of eating anything else made her feel nauseous. How much did she hate her life if she was this much off her food?

The problem was that until the age of 22 Em had known what she was doing with her life – school, 6th form, university and then? For some reason she had never thought what she would do after she had finished all that studying. 'Then' was a complete blank. It was a scary void and she didn't have the faintest idea how to cross it. She had no burning desire to be anything or do anything apart from become an actor, but how was someone with her working-class background supposed to do that? Any time she suggested it, friends and family would laugh at her. She had no training. She had no idea how you became an actor. She didn't even know anyone who worked as one.

After a month or two of twiddling her fingers at home, she managed to wangle a temping job for several months thanks to her best friend, where she spent five days a week sitting in an office, pretending she could type.

When that job came to an end, Em was at a complete loss as to what to do next. Out of desperation she answered an ad for a job as a tourist rep. At least they were looking for people like her with language skills. Em could live abroad and have the chance to speak a foreign language; something she loved doing. Otherwise, she had no real idea what the job entailed. She crossed her fingers that she would be sent to Italy where she had always wanted to live.

As luck would have it, Em never did get to Italy; she was off to Majorca to work for six months. In the run up to her departure date, Em bought herself a Spanish language book and tried to learn some Spanish. She got as far as lesson one and flew off to Majorca armed with that most useful of phrases, 'el campesino trabaja en el campo' – 'the peasant works in the field': a phrase that was sadly destined never to come up in conversation while working there.

This being the mid-1980s, Majorca was full of Brits, Germans, French and Scandinavians; and if the British tourists were anything to go by, tourists came to Majorca for two reasons and two reasons only: it was cheap and sunny. They most definitely did not come because they wanted to experience Spanish culture. The only bit of Spanish culture they wanted to savour was sangria, paella and Spanish beer: at a push maybe watch a flamenco dancer or two.

To accommodate each particular country's foibles, the main strip in the town was divided into a British section, replete with pubs and cafes serving shepherd's pie, fish and chips and Sunday roast dinners; then there were the Scandinavian and French sections and, last but not least, a German section where Em would wisely escape to in order to avoid any chance of bumping into any of the British tourists she was supposed to be responsible for. One of the most surreal moments of her entire time in Majorca had occurred when she sat in 40^0 heat, having 'Kaffee und Kuchen' while a Bavarian Oompah band played in the background. She'd been to Germany on many an occasion and had never experienced anything like it in her life.

Avoiding punters was a top priority, especially when off-duty and, if possible, on-duty as well. For starters, punters were constantly complaining: a regular grumble being that the food was too foreign, despite the hotels serving the blandest hotel food you could imagine. On one memorable occasion a woman complained bitterly to Em that the night before the onion rings had tasted funny. Em didn't have the heart to tell her it was calamari.

Another favourite complaint was that there were too many foreigners. This included those Spaniards who had the temerity to live and work in their own country. Whenever this point was raised, Em would suggest to the complainant that they would be much better off holidaying in Morecombe next year. She would smile sweetly when she said this in the hope that they didn't fully appreciate the loaded sarcasm in her reply. As for her punters' attitude to any German guests who had the nerve to stay in the same hotel as them, well that was another outrage all together. It would seem that informal hostilities had never fully ceased between the two countries despite the Second World War ending 40 odd years ago. A situation exacerbated by the fact that the German guests seemed blissfully unaware of this on-going conflict.

Another common complaint was that the Spanish insisted on speaking Spanish when talking with each other, which seemed to be regarded as the height of bad manners. Em would inform the complainant that the staff were not speaking Spanish: it was Mallorquin. It wasn't; it was Spanish. No Mallorquins worked in the hotel; all the staff seemed to hail from mainland Spain, but the reply would silence the holidaymaker as they tried to figure out exactly what Em was talking about.

Once a punter helpfully pointed out to Em that 'the "foreigners" and I repeat the word "foreigners" (he meant the Germans) should eat after the English'. It was evident that despite the fact he was English and in Spain this particular gentleman did not suspect for one moment that he too might be regarded as a "foreigner". Em took one look at his sunburnt chest, arms and lower legs, his rolled up jeans, his off-white vest and his sun hat, made from a hankie tied in a knot in each corner, and assured him she would have a word with management. What she wanted to say was, 'Look mate, the Germans tip much better than the British; most of the staff here work just 6 months a year: why do you think the waiters head straight for the Germans?' Instead, she sauntered over to reception, speaking loudly in basic Spanish as she went. As soon as the guy was out of ear shot, Em told reception what the guy had said in English (there was no way her Spanish was good enough to explain all that) and they all had a good laugh about it.

The most surprising complaint was when a punter asked Em what number bus he needed to get to Barcelona. He seemed most put out when Em informed him that Majorca was an island and, given the inability of most buses to float, there was no direct bus. 'They could still have a bus,' he observed with a pout. 'Haven't they heard of ferries in Spain?' Em looked him up and down, remembered she had to talk urgently to the head receptionist that very minute and hurried off.

But, all things considered, Em had been lucky. As resorts go, C'an Pastilla was one of the better ones. She was responsible for two hotels: one relatively nice and a much smaller one built over a sewer; its pungent smell filled the rooms on a far too regular basis. The holiday company she worked for knew this, but the hotel was cheap to rent out, so they continued to use it. As a result, Em was called upon to look surprised every time a new coach load of punters turned up at her desk to complain about the various smells. Em would assure them she would inform head office immediately. Needless to say, she never did. What would be the point? They already knew.

Lying to punters was one of her main tasks. Other duties included selling overpriced trips around the island for which she received a tiny commission; being shouted at by furious tourists stuck at the airport every time their flights were delayed, as if she were personally responsible for air traffic control; and not forgetting being shouted at by tourists at the resort who were furious because it was raining, as if she were personally responsible for the weather. All this while constantly avoiding the advances of the coach drivers and those of the head barman at the main hotel. The assumption prevailed among many of the Spanish workers in the tourist industry that all tourist reps were slags, so really what was her problem?

The only light relief came from the guys who worked behind the reception desk at the main hotel where she worked. It was they who made her working life and, by extension, her life, bearable. They were a good laugh: fortunately, they all spoke excellent English, and the back office proved to be a handy refuge if she ever needed to keep a low profile from some punter on a rant. She suspected the Head Receptionist, Antonio, might have a soft spot for her, but he was far too much of a gentleman to do anything about it. She liked him: he was very likeable, but to her 23-year old mind he seemed ancient although he could only have been in his late thirties. In sharp contrast to the unwanted attentions of the head barman, Em appreciated the attention Antonio paid her. Firstly, he gave the impression of genuinely liking her and, most importantly, his manner wasn't in the least bit pushy or threatening.

A month into her new Mallorquin life, Em had struck up a friendship with Sally, a tall, leggy, matchstick-thin, attractive brunette. Sally was a fellow guide who worked for a rival travel company. They had met by pure chance and it was a life saver. Sally hated the job as much as Em, but it was the only job she knew and she was naturally upbeat. Her effervescence was precisely what Em needed. The two women struck gold when they met two sexy Italian tourists and ended up spending the whole week with them. Em, in particular, was infatuated by one of them, a young Roman called Andrea. Sadly, as was customary when it came to Em's love life, nothing romantic happened between them apart from some terrible flirting on her part. On their last night while sitting in a bar, Em noticed that Andrea's mate Davide was wearing two watches.

'Why two watches?' she asked him.

'This one to tell time', he explained and pointed to the watch further up his arm. He then pointed to the watch nearest his hand. 'This one not work, but it go with the jacket.'

Em conceded you couldn't fault the logic. When Andrea and Davide returned back to Rome, life went back to normal. Worse was to follow when Sally was transferred to another island a few weeks later. Em felt as if the small world she had built up for herself had collapsed around her. Friendless and rootless, she found the work increasingly tedious and zombifying; she hated with a passion that she was expected to stay all night at the airport waiting for a bloody airplane to arrive and then be at her desk first thing the next morning. It didn't matter how many hours you worked; the pay remained the same. And the pay was shit.

She was painfully aware too of the reputation that 'guias' had and did her best to ensure that no one got 'the wrong idea'. Meanwhile the head barman was getting more and more arsey the longer he felt she held out. Em knew full well he wasn't particularly attracted to her. She was the new bit of skirt and as head barman he believed he should have first dibs. That was it: a sense of entitlement. The idea that she might not be interested in letting him fuck her didn't enter his head. As far as he was concerned, she was being perverse. Welcome drinks for her punters started to be inexplicably delayed; it was the first stage in what would later become a one-sided war of attrition.

Em soon learned you also had to be on your guard when it came to the coach drivers. If push came to shove, the company would invariably take their side. Late one night, waiting at the airport for yet another airplane to arrive, Em had made the rookie error of having a nap in the back of her coach; when she went to leave, it was clear the driver had no intention of letting her off the coach without her showing her 'gratitude' for the use of his vehicle. His solid form blocked her exit. She had to be careful. She couldn't upset him. If she upset him, he and the other coach drivers would make her life a living hell. Quick as a flash, she decided the only way out was to pretend she thought he was joking. 'Oh, you are funny,' she said in Spanish and punched him with all her might in the stomach. All the time she was laughing and pretending to be joking around. Not expecting the punch, it was hard enough for him to stagger backwards and out of her way. Em jumped down the steps onto the tarmac, still pretending she thought it had all been a huge joke. He never bothered her after that. Maybe he decided if that was a playful punch, what the hell would it be like if she punched him for real?

As a young woman, being harassed in public seemed to be the norm in 80s Spain. Or at least that was Em's experience of living there. Often when she was out and about on her own, she would be catcalled and hissed at as she went along the street. 'Psst, psst guapa' was the sound that would accompany her as she walked. It was so brazen. In London something similar might happen if you passed a building site, otherwise every now and then the odd catcall on the street, usually at night, but on the whole that tended to be it.

But that was nothing compared to the time when, after yet another much delayed late night transfer, she found herself walking home in the early hours of the morning. In theory, the coach drivers were meant to drop her outside her house. In practice, Em was always dropped off at the bottom of her street, irrelevant of how late it was, or the driver would be forced to drive round the houses to get back onto the main road.

That night it was so late that the bar at the bottom of her road was shut. Unfortunately for Em, three scruffy young men, evidently the worse for drink, were still lounging on the bar's veranda. Em passed them, her high heels clomping on the road; she always walked down the middle of the road late at night, never on the pavement. Then they slowly got up and started to follow her. 'Psst, psst guapa', they called after her in between laughing and talking to each other. Em steeled herself not to run. If she ran, they would run too and catch up with her in seconds. She looked around at the houses on both sides of the road, hoping against hope to spot a light on in a window or that some car would drive down the road. Everything was in total darkness. Of course, it was. It was the early hours of the morning; it was a residential area; everyone was sound asleep. She could hear the young men getting closer and closer, laughing and catcalling.

Then, in the distance, she could see a light on in the flat where she lived. She wasn't sure why someone would be up this late, but they evidently were or they had left the light on in the kitchen. Em decided it would be better if the men thought she was Spanish: anything to seem less vulnerable. They might think twice if they thought there was a Spanish father, brother or husband hovering in the background, waiting to 'protect her honour'. If she said the minimum, she could possibly convince them she was Spanish and not some foreigner on her lonesome. 'Jose, venga,' she shouted in the direction of the illuminated window. As soon as she said those two words, she heard the men behind her turn and run off. She had never been so relieved in her life.

A few weeks later, Em was on her way home from the hotel when a car skidded to a stop beside her. She inwardly sighed, fully intending to ignore whatever the driver said. Sure enough, the driver rolled down his window and stuck his head out. She glanced at him from the corner of her eye and realised she recognised him. He was one of the waiters who worked in the hotel restaurant. Manuel. When she'd first learnt his name, she had been tempted to ask him if he'd ever seen Fawlty Towers but quickly dismissed the idea. Her Spanish wasn't good enough. Em had never paid him much attention, given she only saw him at meal times as he went to and fro between the tables. He was always friendly; had an engaging smile and was tall, dark and good-looking. That much she had noticed, but that was about it. All previous conversations between them had been more or less limited to her asking for an 'agua sin gas, por favor' in the hotel restaurant.

'Where are you going?' he asked her in Spanish.

'Home,' Em replied, thankful that it was one of the few questions in Spanish she understood and, more importantly, could answer!

'Fancy a drink?'

Another question she could understand but how to reply? Em's automatic reaction would be to say no and walk off, but for some reason, maybe it was his smile, maybe it was the fact that she hated her life, maybe it was because she felt lost and lonely in this sea of people, she wasn't exactly sure why, but for once in her life she said yes.

'Claro que si.' And she got in the car.

They were soon in a bar in a non-British section of the beach. Thank goodness for that, Em thought. It soon became apparent that Manuel couldn't speak much English and they had to rely on her broken Spanish to get by. 'This is going to be interesting,' she mused. On the plus side, Manuel knew the head barman, so when Em asked for a Bacardi and orange juice, the barman simply placed the bottle of Bacardi in front of her on the bar and told her to help herself. Em did. Several minutes later Manuel and Em were on the dance floor dancing to the latest hit from George Michael, the video to which flashed up on a large screen behind them. Em sang along to *I Want Your Sex*, wondering how good or how bad Manuel's English really was. It was her first night out in ages which didn't involve a trip to the airport. It was also the most fun Em had had since the Italians and Sally had left. Then Manuel leant forward and kissed her. Much to her surprise, Em kissed him back.

This kind of thing never happened to Em. It wasn't that she didn't have admirers. She'd had her fair share of them over the years, but somehow she tended to remain steadfastly in the friend zone. Any possible romance, about to blossom, would somehow wither on the vine. It was as if she had missed the class in school on how to encourage someone to make the first move; or, more importantly, the class on how *she* should make the first move.

It was as if she was paralysed every time by self-doubt. Or maybe it was down to some innate fear of getting close or getting hurt; perhaps it was down to some programmed dread she had that she didn't want people to get the 'wrong idea', whatever 'the wrong idea' was. The wrong idea. Buried deep inside Em was the belief that nothing too bad would happen to her as long as people didn't get 'the wrong idea'. It was her safety net against all the head barmen in the world. After all, as long as people didn't get 'the wrong idea', people would surely be on her side if anything untoward were to happen to her. This was vital in a world where nobody did seem to be on her side; in a world where being harassed was the norm; yet nobody talked about it; everyone ignored and dismissed it; you just dealt with it the best you could and, fingers crossed, nothing too bad would happen to you.

It hadn't been a conscious decision on her part to think like that but it was a form of armour that she had built up around herself through necessity. Whatever the trigger was: self-doubt, fear, naivety, protection, she always tended to keep men at arms' length. Manuel seemed happily unaware of the vibes she was giving off or, if he was, he was singularly ignoring them. Perhaps they got lost in translation. And although she hated to admit it, she kind of liked his manly approach. Call yourself a feminist, she chided herself!

In a yet more surprising turn of events, Manuel stayed the night. Em hadn't taken any notice of him before, yet here he was in her bed. She felt as if she was in a movie, and a fun one at that. In the back of her mind hovered the ghost of the man who she was in love with, but he was in another country, far away, out of reach both physically and emotionally. He'd rejected her time and time again; here was someone in the flesh who wanted her and that in itself was intoxicating.

By the time she had to leave for work the next morning, Em reckoned she must have had about an hour's sleep at most. She was exhausted. Manuel had the morning off, so Em left him sleeping in her bed, while she trudged the 10 long minutes to the hotel. She couldn't remember ever being so tired. As she sat at her desk, all she could think of was getting back to bed and catching up on her sleep. She had never craved sleep the way she did that morning. Everything she did felt as if she was moving through treacle. She was hardly able to string two words together, and gave up any attempt to speak Spanish with the staff. Thank goodness the Spanish had invented siestas and her job was split into morning and evening shifts.

After what seemed an age but was merely a couple of hours, Em made her way home. She assumed Manuel would have long gone by now. All she could think about was bed and sleep. She opened her bedroom door and, to her surprise, Manuel was still there, lying awake in her bed, his hands behind his head. He smiled as she undressed. 'I have to sleep,' she told him in Spanish. 'Only sleep,' she added for extra emphasis. He nodded his agreement as she slipped under the covers. Manuel bent over and kissed her passionately on the mouth. It was as if he had turned on a switch. Em suddenly felt very wide awake. The tiredness that had enveloped her mere seconds before like a sodden blanket evaporated in an instant and she decided that she could always sleep later that night.

That was the start of their relationship. Manuel would come round to her flat almost every evening and on his mornings or afternoons off. They would have fun, chatting, laughing and having sex. Em finally had something to look forward to in her life. Her appetite returned and even her Spanish was improving. Manuel's English not so much despite Em's best efforts.

One night Manuel had asked Em why a hotel guest had called him tall, dark and handsome. He had looked up the words in a dictionary, but for the life of him he couldn't understand why the woman had called him obscuro. 'No, not dark as in a dark room,' Em explained laughingly in Spanish, 'but as in moreno, as in you have dark hair.' This was the problem with small dictionaries. Em knew this from first-hand experience having spent a week in Berlin, aged 14, telling anyone who would listen how 'sexually excited' she was to be in the city instead of 'excited' thanks to her travel dictionary not bothering to specify the subtle difference between 'erregt' and 'aufgeregt'.

The next day Em decided to teach Manuel English, even going so far as to create a little study book for him. It didn't take long for her to give it up as a bad idea. The only sentence Manuel seemed determined to learn in English was 'I am good-looking'. Factually correct, but rather limited on the vocabulary front. The final death knoll to Em's teaching initiative happened one night when they were lying in bed together. Em had her period, was bleeding heavily and feeling sorry for herself.

As she lay in his arms, Manuel kissed her on the shoulder and whispered in her ear, 'Your cunt is bad.' On hearing this, Em wasn't sure whether she should be proud of her teaching skills, the English was grammatically correct after all, or annoyed by the philosophical point he was making. In the end, she laughed out loud.

While she might still be in love with someone else, that someone else didn't want to be with her whereas Manuel did. So much so that he spent all his spare time with her. It all seemed so easy with Manuel while things with the ghost love had all been so complicated. With the latter she would have these earnest conversations that would last until the early hours of the morning; with him she felt she could bear her soul but that didn't stop them from going round and round in circles. Earnest conversations were out with Manuel. They had to be: given they both relied on Em's Spanish to communicate. There was also a clear end date in sight. In two months' time neither of them would be on the island any more. Everything seemed simpler, lighter. After all, it was pointless to take things too seriously when you knew from the start how and when things would end.

Manuel was kind, affectionate, thoughtful and great in bed. He made her happy. Their relationship might be superficial but it was replete with small gestures which made Em smile; which made Em happy. A few weeks into their relationship, having noticed that Em could never find where she put her keys, Manuel brought her a present: a key ring with a massive pink bingo ball attached to it so she could easily locate where she had dumped them. Em laughingly accepted it. That's what Em did more of since she had been with Manuel: she laughed.

Then one of her fellow guides started sticking her oar in, watering the seeds of self-doubt that were always at the back of Em's mind. 'You never go out,' she pointed out to Em. 'You always stay in. Why doesn't he ever take you out? Have you asked yourself that?'

Em hadn't asked herself that, but it was true. They never went out. They did always stay in. The general theory among reps was that if you were dating a Spanish man then somewhere in the background there was bound to be a Spanish 'novia', the girlfriend he was serious about; the woman he was going to marry. The *Guiri* was just for fun. She had never broached the subject with Manuel. Why would she? What if he told her he did have a serious girlfriend? What then? If she had any self-respect, she would have to end things with him on the spot. But the truth was she didn't want to end things. He was the one thing she had to look forward to in her life. At the same time, she hated that she was so pathetic, but consoled herself by reasoning that if Manuel did have a novia, she couldn't possibly live in Majorca. He was always at hers. She refused to give much thought as to why a question of geography should make that much of a difference. It was far better not to think too much about these things, but her friend's comments did what they were meant to do and began to eat away at her.

A couple of days later Manuel popped round as usual. He kicked his shoes off and threw himself onto the bed, his hands behind his head. For once, Em didn't join him, but stood out of arm's reach while she made a big song and dance about the fact that they should go out for once. Manuel lay there and smiled. He seemed fine about the idea. 'Why not?' he replied in Spanish once she'd finished her rant. She had expected him to want to stay in, had been prepared for an argument, but he seemed more than happy to go out, suggesting they drive to a restaurant he knew in the interior, away from all the tourists.

'Muy bien,' she replied and started to get ready. For some reason which Em couldn't quite put her finger on, she felt confused by his reaction. He hadn't minded in the least. Why had she assumed he would? Surely, she should be pleased? It was all so puzzling that Em decided to do what she always did and ignore the thoughts swirling around in her head. She dolled herself up in the bathroom, walked back into her bedroom, looked at Manuel still lounging on top of her bed and it hit her: she was the one who didn't want to go out. If they went out to eat, all she would be thinking about the whole time was when could they get back home and have sex. She didn't want to spend the evening in a bloody restaurant. She wanted to spend the evening having sex with him. Why waste all that bloody time going out when she could sleep with him now?

'I don't want to go out,' Em said in Spanish. 'I want to stay here.' Em sat down next to him and ran her fingers along his chest. 'Vale,' Manuel replied and that was that.

But Manuel had clearly taken Em's minor strop to heart. A week later they went bowling where Em caused consternation by admitting to the man behind the counter that she wore a size 41 shoe. She was promptly told that women's bowling shoes didn't go that high up and she would have to make do with a man's pair. The following week Manuel suggested they head to Palma and go to the cinema. The date movie of choice happened to be The Last Temptation of Christ. Em had hoped the film would be shown in English with Spanish subtitles, but was quickly disabused of that particular piece of wishful thinking. The film was most definitely dubbed into Spanish. Half-way through the film, Manuel asked her if she understood what was going on. It was an understandable concern; Manuel knew how basic Em's Spanish was. Em had hardly understood a word but, as she pointed out to Manuel, she was familiar with the story so she got the gist.

Weeks later they ended up at that restaurant in the island's interior. Besides Em, everyone there was Spanish and the food was divine. It was a big occasion. Manuel was leaving the next day. The hotel they worked in had closed down for the season and he was heading back to La Mancha. Em would be leaving the island for good a week later; it was their last night together.

The two months had sped by. Em still hated her job, but she was going to miss Manuel. But that was that. There was no future for her in Majorca unless she wanted to continue working as a rep and that was not an option. As for Manuel? He was a lovely man; they had fun; all she did was laugh in his company, but she knew so little about him. He lived with an aunt in Palma and he was from La Mancha. That was all she knew. She realised with horror that she didn't even know his last name! She wasn't sure if that said something about her having a shocking lack of interest in other people or more about his sense of privacy. For all she knew there might well be some Spanish girlfriend waiting back home for him in La Mancha, as unaware of Em's existence as she was of hers.

Their final night together flew past at warp speed. As Em dozed in his arms in the early hours of the morning, she wondered if perhaps ending a relationship before it has petered out is for the best. You leave with good memories, wondering what might have been, rather than finishing when it has all gone tits up, bemoaning what it became.

Later that morning Em was still lounging in bed despite the fact she was supposed to be at work. Her hotels might have shut down, but she was scheduled to help out a colleague at a big hotel at the far end of the strip. She was late and toying with the idea of not turning up at all when Manuel joked that she wasn't going to work. As if on cue, Em jumped out of bed and started getting ready. For some reason, his joke had touched a nerve that had become increasingly raw as their last hours together had slipped away and Manuel had singularly failed to suggest they should stay in touch or offered to give her his address. She was damned if she was going to ask him for it. If he didn't want to have anything more to do with her then that was fine by her, although it plainly wasn't.

Meanwhile Manuel was stung to the core as soon as he realised that Em wasn't messing around and was intending to go to work on their last morning together. He too had become steadily more upset by Em's seeming indifference to their imminent separation and that she hadn't mentioned swapping addresses, but he was damned if he was going to give her his address otherwise. If she wanted to keep in touch, she would ask him. At complete cross purposes in their final minutes together, Em kissed Manuel good-bye as nonchalantly as she could manage, and headed off to work. Ironically, it was one of the few times in his company when Em didn't feel in the least like laughing.

As soon as she got to the hotel, she knew she had made a terrible mistake. There was no one about, nothing to do, why the hell was she here? She didn't want to be here; she wanted to be with Manuel. Furious at both herself and at him, she cornered her colleague and asked her for her advice. Without hesitating for a second, her colleague told her she was mad and to piss off back home, she would cover for her. Em jumped into a taxi and hurried back as quickly as she could. Maybe it would be like the morning after their first night together when she returned home from work and found him unexpectedly still lounging in her bed with his hands behind his head. She hoped against hope that would be the case. She made a pact to a God she didn't believe in: if he was still there, she'd tell him how much she liked him and how much she still wanted to keep in touch.

Fumbling at the front door with her key, feeling her stomach turn somersaults with both fear and desire, she let herself into the flat and sprinted the few steps that led from the front door to her bedroom. She opened the bedroom door.

He was gone.

The Lover

The first thing you need to know about any stand up comedian is that every single one of them - without exception - is deluded. You have to be or you'd give up after your first gig. Em was unaware of this axiom at the time, as she looked at the social misfits sitting next to her in a circle under the harsh glare of strip neon lighting in a non-descript room in a community centre in East London. All together there were 8 of them. Herself, a middle-aged woman, soon to be made redundant from a job she hated, who had been treading water all of her life. The fact that she was now unarguably middle-aged and had achieved nothing in her 40 years on the planet had finally hit her and hit her hard.

A kind friend had suggested she try stand up. Em had looked puzzled. 'Stand up?' She'd been to one stand up gig in the 1980s and that had been it. As a form of entertainment, it had never appealed to her.

'Stand up? Why stand up?' She had asked.

'Because you are sitting here crying your eyes out, unable to pick yourself up off the floor to go to work, and you keep making jokes. That's why.'

'Do I?' Em hadn't noticed.

'Yes. If you can make jokes when you're feeling this low maybe you've missed your calling.'

As always, Em had procrastinated, but had eventually given in thanks to her friend's constant nagging and had signed up to do a stand up comedy course. True to form she hadn't done any research on what course was best, but had simply gone for the cheapest and nearest option. That was how she had ended up here.

Sitting next to her was a left-wing political activist who never let a diatribe get in the way of a good joke and a German woman who insisted on writing puns that only made sense if you knew what the words were in German. Em did, but even she had to concede it was niche. There was also a woman with an inferiority complex, who was convinced the world was against her, and whose attempts to manipulate Em were met with cold indifference; a young guy whose confidence and sense of entitlement were in inverse proportion to his talent. On the other hand, he did have the requisite floppy hair encasing a face that Em had to steel herself not to slap. Then there was the middle-aged guy who unlike the others would regularly come up with a good joke or two and seemed pretty normal, so Em was at a loss to understand why exactly he was here; another middle-aged guy who seemed perfectly harmless, but totally unaware of how unfunny he was, and then there was Jack.

Em might be middle-aged with failing eyesight, but she could still appreciate a fine looking man and this one was gorgeous. He was one of the sexiest men she had ever met. She savoured this thought the first time he walked into the room as she desperately tried to keep her mouth closed and forced herself not to dribble. He was tall. She guessed about 6 foot 4. He had sandy hair, perfect bone structure, piercing blue eyes and a body that said there wasn't an inch of fat on him, but, more importantly, that he didn't spend every spare hour in the gym. There were also no visible tattoos. Em hated tattoos, but she suspected in the case of Jack she'd be more than happy to make an exception. He was also funny. He had that knack of telling terrible jokes, but somehow you still laughed at them.

Em concluded that she might not learn much from these stand up comedy classes, but as soon as she saw Jack she knew her money wouldn't be completely wasted. At least she could have a bit of a flirt and Em was a terrible flirt. She would flirt with anyone – as long as she was pretty certain they weren't interested in her or vice versa – why, she even flirted with people she didn't like. Flirting with him was particularly easy. He seemed shy which made him all the sexier. The fact that he had to be in his early twenties and she was 40 – a fact she rarely admitted to, even to herself – meant she was in pretty safe territory. She wouldn't have imagined she stood a chance with him, even if she'd been twenty years younger, but as a middle-aged woman it didn't cross her mind that the flirting would lead to any kind of hook up. Em didn't hook up. She had a wonderful knack of staying in the friend zone even with men she fancied and who fancied her back.

Jack and she had swapped numbers pretty early on. It had been his suggestion. Chatting outside the community centre after class one night, Jack had asked for her number. Em had been so taken aback by the request she had promptly taken a step backward and fallen over a bollard. Jack smiled and chivalrously helped her up; Em secretly hoped he hadn't noticed how heavy she was. He presumably hadn't as he still wanted to swap numbers. That had been several weeks ago and Em had thought no more about it.

Then, one Saturday, Em was out with her mate, faced with that perennial nightmare of finding a decent pair of jeans. Given that most makers of jeans nowadays seem unaware that the average woman doesn't have the athletic build of a pubescent boy, modern jeans were a no-no. Skinny jeans? You have to be kidding! Low waist? Maureen had a stomach and no actual waist and was therefore in dire need of a high waist to at least give the semblance of still having a figure. Thus Em found herself in Camden Market in the hope of finding a vintage pair of dark blue flared jeans from a time when people still made clothing that suited her shape.

After various false starts they had found the exact pair. Grateful at her good fortune, Em ignored the fact that she was paying over the odds for them. 'Could the day get any better?' she mused as she rewarded herself with a cuppa and a slice of cake in a nearby café. Apparently, it could. Em's phone zinged. She picked up her iPhone, managing to get foam from her latte all over the screen. She read the text between the smudges, as a puzzled look spread over her face.

'What's up?' her friend Katrianna asked.

'I just got a text from Jack.'

'Who?'

'Jack, the guy I was telling you about from the comedy class.'

'The good-looking one? What does he say?'

'He wants to come round and visit.'

'Oh, yes', Katrianna replied, giving Em a well-placed nudge. 'I'm sure he does.'

'No, not like that,' Em reassured her.

Not for one second did Em countenance the idea that Jack was suggesting they should have sex, whereas Jack naturally assumed that Em understood that was precisely what he was asking her. Everyone understood the code. Everyone did except for Em.

Em had an all-encompassing blind spot when it came to the dating game. She always had. Em suspected it stemmed from a couple of things. First and foremost, the debilitating lack of self-esteem she had felt as a young woman. She couldn't pinpoint where all that low self-esteem had come from, but it had definitely been instilled in her, as it had been with a lot of young women she knew. On the surface, Em seemed a strong, powerful woman, but the lack of self-worth that lay under the forceful outer veneer tore away at her from the inside, which meant her fall-back position was to assume that men were not attracted to her. It was safer that way.

The second reason was more clear-cut. As a school girl at the tough North London comprehensive she attended, one of her closest friends had been one of the best-looking guys in her year. They both had a similar taste in humour, got on incredibly well and neither fancied the other. It was a perfect friendship. That was apart from one thing. Everyone, everyone at school, everyone in her family, assumed she was sleeping with him. The only one who didn't assume that was her friend's mum who knew for certain they weren't and had a soft spot for Em. This being the 1980s this assumption of her having some casual sexual relationship with one of the best-looking guys at school meant everyone regarded her as a slag. And she paid the price. On two separate occasions, guys at school, guys she had previously considered mates, had tried their luck with her, assuming, as supposed *damaged goods*, they were well within their rights to have a

24

go too, and she had been forced to fight them off tooth and nail. She had determinedly stayed friends with her mate, but her defences were up and thus she always made a show of being 'just good mates' with most of the men in her life. The disadvantage of such a policy was that she also gave that impression to any man she was attracted to.

Katrianna was unaware of her friend's background. Em was adept at giving as little away as possible. Katrianna only knew Em's love life was rather staid, but she'd heard a lot about Jack and assumed Em was being coy. With Katrianna's blessing, Em headed home to tidy up before his arrival and get some biscuits in, Hob Nobs: she wasn't cheap.

Meanwhile, Jack was under the impression he had his night sorted. He'd found out the day before that his girlfriend had cheated on him and he was hurt in a way he'd never felt before. Up until then he had always been the one to cheat. There hadn't been a girlfriend he hadn't cheated on. After all, he was a good-looking guy; he was charming and it wasn't as if he lacked offers. But he had finally thought he'd found the one, and then late last night she'd admitted that she'd fucked someone, though as she pointed out in an attempt to reassure him, she hadn't spent the whole night with the other guy. She'd left as soon as they were done. For once the shoe was on the other foot and he didn't know what to do. He wanted to get back at her and for some reason his thoughts had turned to Em. She was older than him; that was for sure. She was funny and she was attracted to him and he'd never done the older woman thing, so on an impulse he'd texted her. He could sit back and let her take the initiative. At least that was the plan.

He sensed he might have been mistaken about Em's credentials as a woman of the world as soon as she opened the door, standing in the doorway, not in some sexy outfit as he'd imagined, but in jeans and a stripy top, a massive smile plastered on her face asking if he'd like a cup of tea and biscuits. That wasn't quite the start to the grand seduction that he'd been expecting. Em, on the other hand, felt rather pleased with herself as she paraded around in her new purchase. The jeans might have been pricey, but they were flattering. Then much to

Jack's amazement Em showed him into the living room, crowded with books, CDs and DVDs, the TV blaring on in the background and with the overhead light on, bathing the room in the most unromantic of lights. Even more to his surprise they started chatting, he on the sofa, she on the other side of the room, sitting on a shabby office chair by the desk next to the window.

A couple of hours in, Em asked how old he was. '23,' he replied. She looked visibly shaken. 'Why, how old are you?' he asked in turn. '40,' she answered and immediately regretted telling the truth as a look of sheer horror passed over his face, and then for some inexplicable reason they both burst into laughter. 'I thought you were older,' Em said. 'I thought you were younger,' Jack said in return. Something had shifted between them. Neither knew what it was, but for some reason Jack felt he could be honest with her. He began to tell Em about his girlfriend. She seemed genuinely concerned, offering advice on a subject – relationships – she knew little about. Eventually running out of ideas, Em ventured to ask if he had thought of getting laid to get back at his girlfriend.

'Yes,' Jack replied, confused. 'That's why I've come round here.'

'Ah,' Em replied. The penny had dropped. Well, to be fair, it was less the penny dropping, more Em understanding basic English. Normally she would be outraged at the idea that some guy wanted to come round merely to have casual sex with her. She felt she deserved better than that. She stared at him for a moment or two. She had to admit: he was incredibly good-looking. It wasn't every day that a sexy 23 year old was sitting on her sofa asking to have sex with her. She relented. 'I won't shag you, but I'll snog you.' She thought it the most practical of compromises.

Jack smiled his winning smile. 'OK,' and invited Em over to the couch. It didn't take Em long to appreciate how good Jack was at snogging or how much fun it was. The last time she was with a guy, he had not only been that good at it, he had consistently made her feel that she wasn't in the least bit desirable. Jack was the opposite. He made her feel incredibly sexy. Em soon decided it would be far more practical to go into the bedroom, and before long Jack had persuaded her to change into something that showed off her legs and to put on a pair of heels. Em was fine with both suggestions, but given her natural clumsiness was wary at first about putting heels on; it was quite feasible she could have someone's eye out and knowing her luck, it might be her own.

It turned out her plan that they just snog proved an impractical one. Jack proved very persuasive in the best way possible; he was an enthusiastic lover. It wasn't only that he was very good at what he did; his main priority seemed to be to pleasure her. What's not to like? Em realised she was soon making noises that could possibly give a bonobo on heat a run for its money, but when you're having that much fun who the hell cares? She'd also failed to appreciate that a young man's recovery time was a lot faster than men twice their age. She was not only having fun, but lots of it. The whole thing was like movie sex: that El Dorado where the woman enjoys it too. By the end of it all, she'd had so much fun; she had to beg him to stop between her laughter of pure, unadulterated joy.

Then she sensed something had changed. He hadn't said anything. He hadn't moved, but she instinctively knew what was coming next.

'I have to go. She didn't stay the night with her guy and I feel bad if I stayed the night here.'

Em wasn't sure if she should be upset or not. They had already agreed that it was a one off – never to be repeated – and the sex had been off the scale.

'That's fine,' Em said. 'Just promise me two things.'

'What?' Jack asked as he stood up from the bed.

'You text me tomorrow.' Em wasn't sure why she wanted him to do that but she did.

'Fine. And the second thing?'

Em smiled. Jack smiled too and clambered back onto the bed.

The next day Em was horny as hell. She had never been so horny in her life. Jack had texted her as promised and she'd texted back. Her body was crying out for her to ask him round again, but they'd agreed it was a one off thing and so she steeled herself and wrote something bland in reply. As luck would have it a friend called round and helped to take her mind off the fact that she was dying for some more Jack action.

It didn't take long before Em explained the sudden upturn in her sex life.

'What was the sex like?'

'You remember that scene in Thelma and Louise with Brad Pitt?'

'Who doesn't?'

'Like that, but only much, much better.'

'Not possible.'

'Oh yes it was. Several times.'

'Are you going to see him again?'

'No, it was just a one off.'

Of course, it wasn't a one off. Over the next few months Jack and Em became a kind of thing. She didn't kid herself it was going to develop into a relationship: he was far too young and far too fickle, but there was definitely something empowering about having a young, sexy lover while simultaneously not investing any time and energy trying to turn it into something it was never going to be. She knew the relationship had a sell-by date and Em was enjoying the ride for as long as it lasted. As it turned out it didn't last that long, but for someone who 'didn't do casual sex', she had to admit, on this occasion, it had had its benefits.

A year later he visited again. This time another girlfriend, another set of problems. This time they sat on the couch for an age and chatted until Em finally took the initiative and suggested they go into the bedroom. But it wasn't the same. After that she never saw him again.

A true creative, Em decided to use their first night together as a basis for her first stand up routine. That's another thing about stand up comedians: they will use anything in their lives, anything - without exception - as material.

The Austrian

10 years. Em had been single for 10 years. The last time she'd had a boyfriend was February 2001. A decade ago. What's more she was fine about it. She knew such an attitude would never do were she to be the heroine of a film, a novel or a TV series where she was presumably supposed to be waiting for her very own Mr Darcy to appear, while she pretended to get on with her life. But the truth was she wasn't waiting for any grand romance.

According to various tropes that permeate literature, film and television, as a middle-aged, single woman Em should be one of three things: desperate for a man; devoting all her energies to cats or solving crime: think Miss Marple or Jessica Fletcher. Em reckoned that married women – fictional or otherwise - didn't have time to solve crime, because they were no doubt far too busy figuring out how to get away with the perfect murder. Moreover, as an older single woman herself, Em appreciated that the fact that someone died every time Miss Marple or Jessica Fletcher were invited to any social event was a more believable occurrence by far than the likelihood of a single, older woman having been invited to a social event in the first place.

To put it in perspective, Em had been single since before 9/11. In all that time she hadn't managed to find herself a boyfriend, yet during the very same timeframe, the Americans had managed to track down Osama bin Laden and he'd been in hiding! Considering she lived in London, one of the world's major cities with a male population of almost four million, she evidently hadn't been looking very hard.

The problem – well, at least one of them - was that she wasn't attracted to most of the men she met. That wasn't too big a deal, she conceded, as most of the men she met weren't attracted to her. She was middle-aged and overweight. Not the most popular attributes, she presumed, were the average man asked to list what he was most looking for in a woman. Admittedly, she hadn't done the research, but it was a pretty safe bet. In her experience, most men her age wanted to date women in their 20s and 30s. Most men older than her wanted to date women in their 20s and 30s. Most men older than that were dead, but presumably with their dying wish being if only they could date one more woman in their 20s and 30s before they drew their final breath.

Then it happened. She met someone. Manly. Tick. Intelligent. Tick. With an artistic bent. Tick. Handsome. Tick. He looked like the cliché hero of many a romantic novel – not that she read any but she'd seen the covers. He was tall, dark and in great shape despite being in his late 40s. Moreover, he had a wicked sense of humour. The type of Austrian sense of humour she found sexy. Considering she no longer lived in Austria, but was now safely ensconced in a poky flat in North London, it wasn't the best proclivity to have when it came to men. No wonder when she finally came face to face with someone blessed with that particular sense of humour, who also happened to be single, good-looking and seemingly attracted to her, she couldn't help but lap it up.

Mr Seemingly-Perfect was a passing acquaintance of a friend of hers in Vienna. Em's friend had told him to get in touch with Em should he feel at a loss during his week holidaying in London with his three teenage kids. 'You'll like him,' Em's friend had assured her in an email, preparing her for the possible call, and sharing the few scraps of information he knew about him. He was a lot of fun; worked in a gallery in Lower Austria, but only because he had been unable to make it as a painter and needed a steady income once he'd had kids. He was divorced; the kids lived with the ex-wife; and as far as he knew the man was single. That was all he knew. Em Googled him, managed to track down the odd YouTube clip of him talking about art and liked what she saw.

Sure enough he rang and they chatted on the phone. They clicked straight away. Em warmed to his charm immediately. What was it about Austrian charm? Was it the wit? The accent? The intonation? The way with words? Or was it down to the way she associated Austria with much happier times, her youth and good friends?

At one point she asked what he wanted to see in London. Only you, he replied. She laughed down the phone. Of course, that was rubbish. She knew he didn't mean it; he was being charming. Moreover, had a fellow Brit said something that corny to her, she would have told him to stop acting like a twat. Coat such a sentence in the veneer of Austrian charm and with a Viennese accent and she could feel herself falling for it.

Once they met up, it didn't take long for her to confirm that he was divorced and had three children; he worked in a gallery but had a semi-successful sideline in the arts and, most surprisingly of all, he was single, straight and seemed taken with her. They met up a couple of times and kissed rather chastely once or twice. With his charm, wit and good looks, Em had to admit that this particular Austrian did a passable job as a would-be Carry Grant.

Then weeks of separation followed. Luckily, this vast expanse of time was filled by long and witty emails from him and, Em hoped, suitably witty responses from her. His emails made her laugh out loud and reminded her of a time, decades before, when she'd been smitten by another Austrian who used to write regularly to her too. As this had been long before the advent of personal computers, they had sent hand-written letters to each other. Looking back, it all seemed rather quaint. Her current paramour's emails were far wittier than her former beau's epistles. That was for sure, but the emails harked back to the days when people *wrote* to each other rather than merely communicated basic information and a few emojis.

Em suggested some dates when she could go over to Austria to visit. It had been his idea after all. As the weeks began to stretch into months, she had to keep reminding herself of that particular fact. He'd been so quick to mention the possibility of her visiting him that she hadn't had time to drop one of the unsubtle hints on the subject that had been milling about in her head ever since she first met him.

All in all, it seemed the perfect romantic proposal, particularly when he explained that he lived in a small hut on stilts on the banks of the Danube. 'On stilts?' Em queried. 'On account of possible flooding' was his prosaic response. Quickly returning to his charm offensive, he assured her she had nothing to worry about as he would sleep in the garden, flooding permitting. They both laughed at this: both safe in the knowledge that he would do no such thing. Nevertheless, despite his apparent keenness, he kept finding reasons why he wasn't free. The long, humorous emails kept any doubts of Em's at bay. Who would write such long, beautifully worded emails if they weren't interested, Em reasoned.

Moreover, it was the kind of non-relationship Em liked. Technically, she had some romance in her life but it was at a distance. She could spend hours daydreaming about what would eventually happen when they met up; fantasise about how she could work it so she could move to Austria to be with him, but, in reality, she was still single and she could get on with her life as before. Nothing had changed. No compromises were necessary. No adjustments.

Then finally a date was agreed. She was off to Vienna. To meet the man. To meet this Austrian. To meet this artist. To spend the weekend with a guy she didn't know and who, fingers crossed, wasn't some psychotic axe murderer.

He took the day off work (a good sign Em told herself) and he arranged to meet her at Vienna airport. It had been an early flight so she dolled herself up in the airport toilets once they had landed – lenses in, make up on, heels on, hair combed. The intricacies of her toilette meant that she exited ages after everyone else had. By which time, he had almost given up hope of her coming through the doors, an action, delayed even further by her having to keep checking her phone to look at an image of him she'd downloaded from an online art magazine to ensure she walked up to the correct Austrian. For some reason, she couldn't get the image of him stuck in her head. Diplomacy dictated (or rather her best mate Christine had pointed out) it was best to forego the option of having the phone in her hand, checking his image, as she approached him.

As luck would have it, or possibly Google images, Em walked up to the correct Austrian. They kissed and they headed to his. They stopped off to buy food, visited some famous hill, where they kissed again among the flower blossom and then set out for his house by the Danube. It was weird. She had lived in Vienna several times over the years and had rarely seen the river so synonymous with the Austrian capital.

They had lunch, chatted over coffee and then he indicated with his head that they should go upstairs. For once he seemed lost for words.

'You must be tired,' he said. 'You could probably do with a nap.'

Being middle-aged, she wasn't sure if he was being coy or suggesting a pastime which she regularly enjoyed now she was in her 'prime'.

'Erm, yes,' Em replied. Not sure what she was agreeing too.

The attic bedroom was sparse. On either side of the stairs that led up into the bedroom lay a mattress on the floor. A king size mattress lay to the right, facing a large TV while on the other side of the stairs lay a single mattress.

Both Em and the Austrian seemed embarrassed by the situation. Em decided to take the initiative and plonked herself on the double mattress. She hoped it was in a vamp-like manner, but given that the mattress was on the floor and she was not as lithe as she used to be she wasn't convinced she'd been that successful.

This seemed to be the case as her would-be lover opted for the single mattress on the other side of the stairs. Em reassured him that he'd be perfectly safe and he should come over to her. By this point, Em wasn't sure if he was being a gentleman or if she had seriously miscalculated what this weekend was about.

Fortunately, he didn't need much encouragement: he sauntered over and dropped onto the mattress beside her. A few minutes later his arm was wrapped around her body as he apparently snoozed. She decided to take the initiative by caressing one of his fingers. In her head she might see herself as a vamp, but the sad truth was that she acted more like someone who had learnt romance from watching one too many Ivory Merchant movies. Even she recognised that perhaps it was not the greatest sign of encouragement a would-be lover has ever shown to the object of their affection, but it got the ball rolling. Things progressed to such an extent that Em was in the throes of passion when her phone started ringing and the Best of My Love by The Emotions blared out between her moans.

Never had Em wished so much with all her heart that she'd switched her phone off. Given the state of play, Em and the Austrian ignored the music until seconds later Em's phone started ringing again. Em knew at once who it would be: her best friend, Christine. She wouldn't stop ringing until she answered the bloody thing. Em couldn't believe her luck. She'd had no sex for years. For bloody years. And it was at this precise moment that Christine chose to call her.

It transpired that Christine had taken Em's joke about the Austrian being a possible serial killer to heart, and had decided to check in on her to make sure that her friend wasn't about to be killed. Em would have liked to point out that if Austrian man had been about to kill her, he probably wouldn't have allowed her to answer the phone, let alone allow her to inform Christine of his plans, but given that the Austrian spoke fluent English she was limited as to how she could respond.

'Are you OK?' Christine asked.

'I'm in Austria. Don't you remember?' Em replied, looking at the Austrian, as if to say what is she like.

'Are you all right? Can you speak?' Christine asked again, her flair for the dramatic getting the better of her.

'Yes, of course I can. I'll call you later.' And before Christine could suggest she should text her some kind of coded message, Em hung up. This time Em was taking no chances and switched the phone off.

**

Later that evening they went to a Heuriger, perched on top of a hill, with a great view of the Lower Austrian countryside unfolding before it. The Austrian might be a few years older than Em but he was unquestionably fitter. Em knew from their previous conversations that in his spare time he climbed hills, swam regularly and went for long walks through the glorious Austrian countryside, whereas being a city girl through and through, Em didn't do any of those activities. She never as much as took the stairs if a lift or escalator was an option, even if she was going *down* a floor. This meant that what was supposed to be a romantic walk up a hill for the Austrian was a heart-attack inducing climb up a mountain for Em who, a few seconds in, was panting heavily and apparently in need of an oxygen mask. The Austrian looked on in amazement. Em wondered whether turning puce really brought out her features.

Finally, they made it to the top and the view was spectacular. As the night set in, it became more and more romantic, particularly once Em had stopped wheezing. It would have been a perfectly romantic evening but for one thing. She noticed that the Austrian liked to flirt in front of her. She wasn't sure if it was to make her jealous or he couldn't help himself. She had observed that it seemed to be a 'thing' that quite a few men did nowadays. As if they'd read it in some book somewhere. Make them jealous, keep them keen. It had the opposite effect on her: it just made her want to tell them to piss off. But given she was staying at his and she was far too mean to pay for a hotel that wasn't an option.

The object of his flirtation was their waitress. She was in her twenties, dressed in regulation black, slim, with a mane of curly brown hair flowing down her back. She was young and beautiful. Moreover, she was a happy soul. Em soon picked up she had an accent. It didn't take her long to learn that the waitress hailed from Italy, whose language Em spoke fluently. Quick as a flash, Em started chatting to her in Italian, befriending her immediately and ensuring that the Austrian played second fiddle in their conversation. Em was pleased with herself, some might call it smug, that she had dealt with the situation so adroitly, but the first crack had appeared. If only she hadn't been so determined to convince herself that he was *the one*, she might have noticed.

***

The next crack didn't take too long to make an appearance either. In the early hours of the next day, 6 am to be exact, there was a loud banging on the front door. The banging, it turned out, was thanks to the Austrian's ex-wife who had left her car in Vienna the night before, yet had somehow managed to get back to this particular sleepy village by the Danube and now needed her ex to give her a lift back into town.

Thanks to being half asleep Em didn't ask too many questions, though an hour and half later when he still hadn't returned, they began to filter through her head, as she lounged in bed. Why had the wife left her car in Vienna? Why did *he* have to drive her there for her to pick her car up? And given that Austria had a fantastic public transport system why didn't she make use of it? Em suspected the ex-wife was making her presence felt and for once her suspicion was right.

Hours later, ex-wife safely deposited in Vienna, late lunch served, mobile phones switched off, Em was enjoying some afternoon delight take 2 when the front door below thudded open and heavy footsteps could be heard running up the stairs. For a second it flashed through Em's mind that Christine had somehow managed to track her down. Em wouldn't put it past her. Christine could be a very determined woman once she put her mind to something.

The Austrian had evidently a better idea of who it could be.

'Go back down', he said in German. 'We're coming.'

If only, Em thought.

The Austrian dressed quickly and hurried downstairs after whispering into Em's ear, 'It's the kids.'

Em knew he had three of them but hadn't expected to see them. Most single parents she knew didn't let their kids go anywhere near anyone they were seeing unless they were sure it was serious. Ergo: he must be serious about her. It was logic like this that enabled Em to appraise a situation to her advantage without any thought to the reality of what was going on.

Minutes later, Em made her way down the stairs, conscious that she had sex hair and that the kids must have guessed what had been going on. The two daughters seemed to have a pretty good idea. The son seemed unusually naïve for his age.

'Why were you upstairs?' he asked innocently. 'It's the afternoon.' Em looked at the floor. They were his kids. He could deal with that one.

'The weather wasn't that good earlier so we decided to watch some telly.' Their father answered so convincingly that for a second Em was half convinced that had been the reason. No one deemed it necessary to point out that the telly hadn't been switched on.

The Austrian ushered everyone outside onto the porch, having noticed that the weather had taken a distinct turn for the better. Sitting in the sun, they enjoyed a lively chat over coffee and cake. His children were a lot of fun and, as was her wont with kids and young adults, Em got on with them famously. As far as they were concerned, she had won major Brownie points back in London for having arranged free tickets to Madame Tussauds for the family during their stay there.

It was soon decided they would go canoeing on the river.

'You're coming, aren't you?' asked the son. 'There's room in the canoe.'

Em looked down at her red and white striped cocktail dress which, given the colours and the country she was in, seemed rather patriotic of her, and then over to her red stiletto heels that she had kicked off by the door.

'I don't think so. I'll come with you and then go for a coffee while you're on the river and meet you all afterwards.'

No time was lost in getting the canoe out from underneath the house. Em volunteered to help carry the canoe to the river. It didn't take her long to realise how bloody heavy it was. But these were early days in a possible relationship, thus she needed to give the impression of being a helpful, nice person and said nothing. Her natural instinct would have been to leave them to it.

They passed by his neighbour's hut. The owner, a woman in her late-30s with spiky pink hair, dressed in a t-shirt and jeans, was sitting on the porch, drinking from a dainty cup, a cigarette curling smoke in the ashtray in front of her.

'Grüß Gott,' Em said as they passed by, smiling in the woman's direction. She had assumed everyone would say hello. Particularly in a small place like this. Yet there was stony silence from all the Austrians including the neighbour who glared at Em, snatched up the ashtray and stomped inside the hut.

'What's wrong with her?' Em asked.

'She's a bit strange,' the Austrian replied, as his eyes darted to the hut, then his children, to Em, and then back to the hut they had just passed. Realising that Em was staring at him, he broke out in a big smile. 'Ignore her. That's what I always do.'

'Oh, OK.'

Em guessed there was more to it. The woman had looked furious. However, as the children were with them, she decided to leave it for now. Finally, they got to the water's edge.

'I'll see you in an hour,' Em told them. 'I'll be in the café. Have fun!' Em turned on her heels and spent the next hour drinking coffee and glancing through two newspapers and several magazines.

Sure enough, an hour later, the Austrian had returned.

'Where are the kids?' Em asked.

'They're taking the canoe back.'

Em's first reaction was to marvel at the apparent upper arm strength of the average Austrian young person.

'I've told them to go back home so we can spend the rest of the day together. Just the two of us,' he added. The Austrian smiled, sat down, called over the waiter and ordered himself a Brauner and another Melange for Em. He seemed unusually quiet.

'Why is your neighbour so unfriendly?' Em asked, trying to break the ice.

'No idea.'

'Has she always been like that?'

'More or less.'

Before Em could probe any further, he was on the offensive.

'You could have watched us, you know. I mean, on the river.' He sounded hurt.

'I'm not spending a whole hour watching you and the kids canoe up and down the Danube,' Em replied. She knew she had to seem nicer than she really was but there were limits.

'You could have watched us sail off at least,' he replied.

Em was silent. He had a point. It hadn't even crossed her mind.

∗∗∗

What did cross her mind half an hour later was that the Austrian had forgotten his wallet. There had been some rigmarole with his credit card the first time they had gone out together in London when it looked for one scary moment that she would have to pay for all the drinks. She had insisted they go Dutch last night and, much to her surprise, he hadn't put up any kind of argument on that score. Today he'd forgotten his wallet. There was a pattern developing here.

Later that evening they headed into Vienna to see a film but unable to decide on what to see they soon headed back home. Em imagined a romantic evening was in store for them, but she could sense he was making less and less of an effort. Or maybe those rose-tinted glasses of hers were letting in more of the light.

They started to watch an Austrian film on the telly. Em tried to make him understand that as the film was mainly in dialect, the only dialogue she understood were the words 'Servus' and 'Pfiat di' in other words hello and bye. This meant that trying to understand what the hell was going on was proving impossible for her. The Austrian was adamant that her Austrian German was good enough. Em silently wondered to herself if her Austrian German was so bloody good, why he didn't understand the point she was making.

She decided to try another tack and be pro-active by initiating a few romantic manoeuvres. At first, he seemed responsive and keen. The TV was switched off, smooching was in full flow, and Em was wondering who would interrupt them first: Christine parachuting in, the kids arriving for another chat or the ex-wife with some half-baked reason why he had to leave the house with her.

What she hadn't factored in was that he himself would bring a halt to proceedings. All of a sudden, before things really got started, he declared he was tired, kissed her on the lips and rolled over on his side.

Em wasn't sure what had happened. She sat upright for a minute or two. She had begun to suspect that he was a ladies' man and only interested in the chase; and now he'd *caught* her, the interest was waning quickly. Either that or the more time he spent with her, the less attracted he was to her. She soon put that thought to the back of her mind. There was absolutely no need to be that honest with oneself. Mind you, if he were a ladies' man then surely he was after sex. It went without saying that if she had thought that from the start, she would have been highly insulted. Now it looked as if he wasn't even interested in her for the sex. It dawned on Em that was by far a much worse scenario.

She had three options. She could go into vamp mode and seduce him but that didn't appeal. She couldn't face the possible rejection. Alternatively, she could be an adult and talk to him about it. She knew herself well enough to know that was never going to happen. Thirdly, she could pretend it didn't bother her and ignore the situation. It had been a reaction she'd learnt during her days at school when she had been constantly bullied. Ignore them and they will stop was the mantra she'd been told as a child. That's what she did. If someone hurt her, she would pretend it didn't bother her; that it wasn't important to her. As a strategy, it had never worked. It never *did* stop the bullies. It didn't work now, but it was still her instinctive reaction despite its proven lack of efficacy. She shrugged her shoulders, lay down and after a while drifted into sleep.

***

It had been decided they would spend Sunday afternoon visiting the art gallery where he worked. There was a special exhibition on, featuring artists from Lower Austria which, for the sake of their romance, Em pretended to be interested in. Unfortunately, the exhibition proved to be much larger than she thought it would be when he'd first suggested it. How many artists were there in Lower Austria for heaven's sake? Em wasn't sure that her approach to art appreciation was the correct one, but for her when she looked at 'art', she had to feel as if she were taken aback by the skill, the imagination, the creativity, the wonder that another human being could create something like that. Something that she was unable to create, that was beyond her ken. The art works here left her singularly uninspired.

'I'm working on something at the moment. Do you want to see it?'

Em presumed it was a rhetorical question but nonetheless replied in the affirmative.

Nodding at a warden who looked so bored that Em suspected death would be a welcome release, the Austrian buzzed open a door and suddenly she was being led down a maze of corridors and into a room which the Austrian informed her was his office. Em was impressed. His office was about twice the size of her London flat. In one corner there stood a canvas on an easel. It was half finished but it was evident from a mere glance that the Austrian had talent. Em moved closer to the painting. It didn't leave much to the imagination. The body of a young, naked woman lay on a wooden floor in a pool of light. The woman was beautiful, slim, with long limbs and a mass of blonde hair which swirled round her head and down over her shoulders. What hit you were the reds which suffused the surface of the painting. You had the impression that a lot of passion had gone into the painting of it. It was the most erotic sign he'd given her all weekend.

Em stepped even closer. She dreaded to think how she'd look if he painted her. Apart from the fact that her body was definitely not as lithesome as the model's depicted on the canvas, other confidence-threatening issues had arisen during her visit. Back in London, the idea of staying in a hut on stilts by the river had sounded romantic, but she'd forgotten to factor in that warm weather in combination with water equals midges and it transpired that the midges of the Danube were partial to her. At the moment she had a bite on both her forehead and left arm, both of which had reacted by coming out in what looked like boils. It wasn't the greatest of looks.

'What do you think?' He asked. He seemed genuinely interested in her opinion.

'It's good. It's really good. I …' but Em didn't have time to tell him what she thought.

The door opened and a young woman entered the room. There could be no mistaking who she was. She had to be the model who had sat for his painting, and in real life she looked all the more glorious. She was tall, very tall. Em reckoned she reached about 6 foot high at the very least, and that was without heels on. Not too thin, her body was in perfect proportion to her height. The main difference to her painted image was that her blonde mane was tied back in a ponytail, secured with a bright purple ribbon that matched the sundress which swirled around her as she walked towards them.

'Hi,' she smiled and planted a kiss on the Austrian's cheeks.

'This is Em,' the Austrian said, giving the young woman a knowing look. 'I didn't realise you would be here.' He turned to Em, 'This is Dominique. A work colleague of mine.'

Em and Dominique shook hands as Em became painfully aware how much younger and how much more attractive Dominique was close up.

'Your bra strap is showing!' The Austrian noted and with that he started fidgeting with the bra strap on Dominique's shoulder. Dominique giggled and allowed him to fiddle around with her bra. Em couldn't believe it. She'd been in his bed a mere two hours earlier and now he was playing with some woman's underwear right in front of her.

'I'm off,' Em snapped and stomped out of the room before anyone could say anything. Seconds later she stomped back in again having realised she had no idea how to get out of the building.

'Sorry,' she said through pursed lips. 'You'll need to show me how to get out of here. *Now*, please. I need to meet my friend.'

The Austrian looked taken aback. Dominique looked bemused. Em was trying to stay calm but she had a temper that was hard to conceal at the best of times. It was one of the things she had inherited from her mother, along with a wart on the side of her head which fortunately was covered by her hair.

More subdued than normal, the Austrian led her along the maze of corridors.

'Who are you meeting?' the Austrian asked. 'You never said.'

'A friend,' Em lied.

'Shall I come with you?'

'No, it's probably best if I meet you later. You stay here. I'm sure you have lots of work to do. I'll text you.'

Em turned on her heels and made her way out of the gallery, gasping for air. What the hell was she going to do now? Those two had clearly been an item at some point. You could tell. Maybe they were still an item. What an idiot she had been! She had let her imagination run away with her, and had turned the morsels he had handed her into a cake. She had been bowled over by his charm and wit but there had been nothing of substance – just a far too vivid imagination on her part.

She had to do something. She made her way to the café opposite, ordered an Einspänner, a coffee smothered in whipped cream. It had been her comfort drink of choice when a youth in Vienna, and she told herself she deserved a treat. Then she called Robert, a former flatmate from her student days in Vienna. A funny, lovely bloke. He had moved to Lower Austria in the 90s. Despite the fact they'd only been flatmates for four months decades ago, they were still good friends. She had no idea if the village he lived in was anywhere near where she was, but she could ask and see if he could meet up. It was a big ask but he was that kind of guy.

Sure enough, two Einspänners and three Topfenschnitten later, Robert was sitting opposite her, ordering a beer. Em recounted in minute detail her latest romantic misadventure. Robert did as he always had done: he listened while at the same time wondering why Em always made the same mistakes and why she always had such chronic bad taste in men. Every now and then, he'd crack the odd joke and Em's face would lighten up as she laughed. Ten minutes later even Em had got bored with the subject, and they began to relive former memories of their student days when all of a sudden Robert stopped speaking, raised an eyebrow and nodded his head. Em instinctively looked round and spotted the Austrian standing behind her.

'I wondered where you'd got to,' he said as he sat down to join them and ordered a Brauner. 'You never texted.'

'Didn't I? I told you I was meeting a friend. This is Robert, by the way.'

Robert smiled while trying to come up with an exit plan. The desultory conversation dragged on for another 15 minutes or so until Robert made his excuses and insisted on paying the bill, much to the relief of both the Austrian and Em. Em got up, gave Robert a massive hug and asked him to send her love to his wife and kids.

'Sure,' he replied as he smiled at her in encouragement.

Em sat down again and stared at the Austrian. He seemed to be on another charm offensive, but this time Em could see through it in a way she had been unable to do so before. Then the doubts began to surface. Had she overreacted? Had she made a mountain out of a molehill? Then again, playing with someone's bra strap was quite an intimate thing to do. Did it really matter though? She very much doubted he would want to meet up again, and she had a sneaking suspicion she wasn't that keen herself. Out of some masochistic sense of curiosity she thought she'd check out the lay of the land.

'So, when do you fancy meeting up again?' she asked as she played with her teaspoon.

He hesitated for a second, taken aback by her bluntness, and then smiled at her.

'Sometime next year?' He said jokingly and then rushed to reassure her. 'I'm really busy at work at the moment, what with the exhibition and everything, but once things calm down a little. I can't say when for definite though. Not right now.'

In other words, never, Em thought to herself.

'Totally understand,' she replied. 'Shall we have some food while we are here?'

A veneer of unease had engulfed them by now. Both knew it and both steadfastly refused to mention it. Em made the most of the situation and ordered one of her favourite meals: goulash with bread dumplings and for afters a large portion of Kaiserschmarrn. There is, after all, nothing like carbs (besides chocolate) to placate a breaking heart. That and petty victories. She managed to score one, enjoying the look on his face when she informed him that she'd left her purse at home and he had to foot the bill. Yes, it was petty of her, she knew, but then again all is fair in love and war.

On the way home the atmosphere eased somewhat as they discussed art, taking turns to enthuse about those artists who meant the most to them. Em wondered if this conversation was the most genuine he'd been with her all weekend. It seemed they both had silently agreed not to mention the whys and wherefores of Em storming out of the gallery earlier. But what to do about tonight? Did she want to sleep with him? Given that she never dated, rarely met men that she found attractive enough that she wanted to sleep with them, the chances of her having another sexual encounter in the foreseeable future were remote. Should she make the most of it while she had the chance? How romantic was that? Then again, did he want to sleep with her? He hadn't been that amorous last night after all.

As they arrived back at his riverside hut, it seemed any decision would have to wait as Em spotted his wife sitting on the bench on the porch. Em and the wife smiled at each other and shook hands as they said hello. The wife explained she needed his signature for some school trip the two youngest children were undertaking and apparently there was no time like the present. Em wasn't sure if this was another example of the ex-wife marking out her territory or yet another case of annoying Austrian bureaucracy coming to the fore. Nor did she care.

'Nice to meet you,' she lied, smiling at the wife. 'I'll leave you to it,' Em informed them as she made her way upstairs. 'I have an early flight tomorrow.'

Thirty minutes later Em heard the ex-wife drive off as the Austrian called out her name from the foot of the stairs. Em put down the watch that she had been avidly looking at since she'd been in the bedroom, awaiting the ex-wife's departure: every passing minute another stab to her heart; more fuel on the fire of her anger. As soon as she'd put the watch on the floor beside her, her head hit the pillow and she feigned sleep. She felt it was the easiest option. Shortly afterwards the Austrian tiptoed into the room. Whether he knew Em was pretending to sleep or not, he seemed happy to go along with it. He undressed, slipped into the bed beside her; and, much to Em's annoyance, he soon fell asleep.

Em lay there. She was half relieved that he hadn't tried to 'waken' her while at the same time half insulted that he hadn't. So much for him finding her attractive. So much for a dirty weekend. At heart, she was angry with herself. She knew only too well that she was partly to blame for the situation she was in. She'd read far too much into it from the start. After all, she might find it difficult to find someone she was attracted to; it didn't mean he had the same problem. Unlike her, he didn't seem short of admirers. Dominique was attracted to him; that was for sure. The Italian waitress hadn't been averse to his overtures. She was convinced that something had gone on with the neighbour and as for the ex-wife? She was still hanging around. And that was just the women she knew about! And she'd only been here a couple of days! He was a good-looking man, witty and charming. He presumably hadn't viewed their getting together as a big deal. He'd never said as such. That had been all her – her imagination, her wishful thinking, her reading too much grand literature or watching too many Cary Grant films when that *is* what happens.

She tossed and turned and started to worry she might wake him up. She got out of bed, took the duvet from the other bed and headed downstairs to sleep on the sofa downstairs. Sleep evaded her for what seemed like ages but she must have nodded off at some point because the next thing she knew the Austrian was standing over her, calling her name and lightly shaking her shoulder.

'What are you doing down here?' he asked, smiling.

'I couldn't sleep and I didn't want to wake you up. What time is it?'

'Only 6. Do you want to go back to bed and I'll make us some coffee.'

The charm was back on then. Coffee was served, followed by a bit of smooching and avowals by the Austrian that they would meet up soon, although Em noted it was all very vague. What he wasn't vague about was that he could no longer take her to the airport. Something had come up, some meeting or other but he could drop her off at the station and she could get a train to the airport from there. Em was about to cast aspersions as to the likelihood of him just finding out about this meeting but bit her tongue. What was the point? 'Fine,' she said. She grabbed her toilet bag and headed downstairs for the shower.

***

They had kissed in the car and Em got out and went to grab her suitcase. Ever the Viennese gentleman, he got out the car too and took her suitcase out of the boot for her. They hugged. Em could see he looked anxious. Maybe he was worried she would make some embarrassing declaration. He must know she was pissed off. She didn't have a poker face at the best of times, but she did her best, and cheerfully said good-bye and headed off to the station without once looking back.

As the weeks passed, his emails continued. Long, incredibly long emails, full of humour and excuses as to why he couldn't come to London just yet. Em continued to reply, but she wasn't sure why. The writing had been writ large on the wall, but there was a part of her that hoped against hope that she had read it all wrong. What was that about? Why was that? Why be in such denial? It wasn't as if she hadn't experienced that kind of pointless, self-lacerating hope with men before. All it did was drag out the inevitable and make you feel worse about yourself. Nevertheless, the electronic correspondence continued as the weeks turned into months. A Christmas card arrived. Em noticed the card was gallery issue and he'd had it franked at work so he hadn't even had to splash out on the cost of a stamp. He texted her in the New Year to ask if he could call her. 'Of course, you can,' she'd replied. He never rang.

A month later, she had to go to Vienna for work. She emailed him. He'd love to meet up. They made plans to meet at a café in the first district. Despite her best intentions, she counted down the days till they would meet.

She kidded herself that she was now immune to his charms. She still told herself that while she got her hair cut and blow-dried and had a bikini wax the day before she left on her work trip. She still told herself that in the hour before their date, as she applied her make up in a far less haphazard fashion than usual. As she closed her hotel room door, she looked at the double bed. Would she bring him back? Should she bring him back? The answer was obviously: NO. She knew that, of course, but she feared that she might. Seriously, what was that about? Low self-esteem? Desperation? Trying to prove to yourself that he was *the one* after all? That you had been right all along? She hated that she acted like this but she seemed to lack the tools or the mental discipline to act otherwise.

After a short walk in crippling high heels, she was sat at a table, enjoying a mojito, looking at her watch. It was five to nine. They were supposed to meet at nine. If he wasn't there by quarter past, she was off. Em tried to look away from the flight of stairs that led down to the bar but she couldn't help herself. Her heart suddenly missed a beat. She could hear someone coming down the stairs, but then she spotted two sets of feet – one set belonging to a man, the other to a woman. So that definitely wasn't him then. She involuntarily slumped back in her seat. Then the legs came into view, then the top half of the bodies and then their faces. That was when the pit of her stomach fell to the floor. It was him all right and he was with a date.

The date in question looked to be in her late 40s, another blond; blue-eyed, attractive, elegantly dressed and evidently besotted with the Austrian. For his part, he seemed embarrassed by the situation. The woman seemed pleasant enough and presumably had no idea who Em was. Em's mind darted back for a second to the Austrian's unfriendly neighbour. She never had gotten to the bottom of that particular story but suspected she'd unintentionally repeated it.

What was he hoping? To make the date jealous? To make her jealous? To cause them both pain? To have them fight over him? Em did wonder about her self-esteem at times, but it wasn't that low.

'Sorry. I need to go. I just got a text from Robert. Trouble with the wife. I have to meet him at Westbahnhof,' Em lied once more, impressed by her quick thinking.

'What right now?' the Austrian asked.

'Yes, it's an emergency. Sorry, I just got the text.'

Em waved her phone in the air as if to confirm the veracity of what she had said. She rooted around in her purse for some cash and slapped it on the table.

'That's for my drink.'

Em wanted to warn his date, tell her to make a run for it, but what would be the point. She wouldn't believe her. She'd have to find out for herself. Just as she had.

'How long are you in Vienna for?' the Austrian asked.

'I have to leave tomorrow for Innsbruck, and then I fly back to the UK from there.'

Another lie but what did it matter. He could hardly check.

'Maybe we can meet up properly the next time I'm here for work. I'll email you when I'm next in town. Really sorry, but Robert sounded so upset. Bye.'

Em grabbed her bag, smiled at the date, got up, walked up the stairs and never looked back.

After a period of radio silence, out of the blue he emailed her to apologise for his behaviour, and to let her know how embarrassing it had been for *him. For him!* Em decided she had nothing to say to him, and never replied back, safe in the knowledge that her ignoring him might dent his ego a bit, but nothing else.

Months later she was back in Vienna for work, and would have to stay there for a couple of weeks. She never did email. She didn't call. It was only when Robert mentioned him in passing one night when she was staying with him and his family that it hit her: she really had become immune to his charms.

The Bell End

Why was it that friends in possession of a partner almost invariably lacked good sense? Over the years Em had come to this conclusion as she watched more and more of her friends settle down with utter bell ends. Yes, to be sure there were exceptions to this rule: some friends had chosen wisely, but it seemed to Em that when it came to her close friends, they always had awful taste when it came to men. No more so than her best friend, Alice.

As far as Em was concerned, Alice's boyfriend Mark was a massive bell end. Obviously, you can't go up to people and tell them they are massive bell ends: that's considered rude. This was why Em had been politely asked by Alice to stop doing that. Given Em's forthright personality, it had been somewhat difficult for her to refrain from speaking her mind but, then again, Alice was her best friend so Em forced herself not to voice her opinion about Mark – at least to his face. It didn't stop her thinking it though.

Try as she might, Em couldn't see what Alice saw in him. Alice had a winning personality, a good heart, was attractive and had a great figure to boot; her dress style might be a bit kooky but she always looked great. The overall effect was that she looked a lot younger than 36. Besides her physical attributes, Alice was charming, had a successful job in the media, was constantly meeting new people and wasn't short of admirers, but for some reason Alice had fallen for Mark.

Begrudgingly, Em had to admit Mark was handsome but he irritated the hell out of her. He was one of those insecure men who try to make themselves feel better by chipping away at the self-esteem of others, particularly when it comes to the women in his life. Em had been out with a guy like that herself a decade ago and, instinctively, her hackles were raised as soon as she experienced any similar behaviour either towards herself or her friends.

Weeks earlier, Mark had 'forbidden' Alice from reading any novels until she'd finished a book of short stories that he'd recommended Alice read.

'What the fuck are you on about?' Em justifiably asked as soon as she'd heard. 'Alice can read what the hell she likes.'

'No', Mark countered, 'she should read these first before she goes on to reading a novel.'

'Why? It's some new law, is it? You can't read a novel until you've read a set amount of short stories? I'm currently reading Quiet Flows the Don. You're lucky you're not saying this to me as there's a very good chance that I'd hit you over the head with it.'

To prove her point, Em rummaged in her handbag and took out a dog-eared copy of the rather sturdy book in question and vigorously shook it in the air.

'It makes sense in a way,' Alice said in a vain attempt to keep the peace, slightly unsure as to whether Em was planning on throwing this particular fine example of Soviet literature at her fiancé's head.

'No, it doesn't.'

'She hasn't finished the short stories yet,' Mark explained.

'Maybe she doesn't enjoy reading them.'

'Mark is very well read,' Alice intervened on Mark's behalf.

'So am I. I still don't tell you what you can and can't read though.'

'You've only got to look at my collection,' Mark said, pointing at the overstuffed bookshelves next to him, 'Marquez, Kerouac, Bukowski, Dostoyevsky, Joyce, Allende.'

Unfortunately for Mark, he had fallen into the trap of pronouncing Allende as the average English person was wont to, given their ingrained aversion to learning foreign languages, rather than pronouncing the author's surname the Spanish way. Knowing Mark would be annoyed if she corrected him, Em immediately did. After all, Em would be the first to admit she could be petty when the need arose. In her defence, if Mark was going to pretend to be an intellectual then he could at least get his Spanish pronunciation right.

'Ayende, I'll think you'll find it is pronounced Ayende,' Em retorted while, much to Alice's relief, Em placed her novel back into her handbag.

Mark said nothing. Annoyingly he knew Em would be right so he tried to get his own back by prophesying, incorrectly as it turned out, that Andy Murray would lose the Wimbledon Men's Singles Final, scheduled for the next day. Aware that Em was proud of her Scottish roots, he hoped that this attempt at being the voice of doom with regard to Andy Murray's tennis skills would upset her national pride.

Unfortunately for Mark, he had failed to take into consideration that Em didn't care what Mark thought about anything, least of all his assessment of Andy Murray. Em managed instead to wind Mark up by pretending she wasn't listening to what he was saying, being far too busy playing with her phone, by texting 'Jesus wept. Alice's boyfriend is a bell end' to as many friends as she could think of. It had taken Mark much longer than she had thought possible for him to cotton on to what she was up to. When the penny finally dropped, he stomped off upstairs leaving Em and Alice to catch up on all their latest news. Alice, ever the diplomat, always chose to ignore Mark and Em's little spats.

Em appreciated that Alice's biological clock was ticking and that she desperately wanted to be a mum: presumably Mark had arrived on the scene just in the nick of time, but surely remaining childless was a far better option than being in a relationship with a bell end. Em felt, and with good reason, it was remarks like that which had prevented Alice asking her to be bridesmaid at their forthcoming wedding. Em reflected that she should have been insulted by this oversight by her best friend on what is supposedly the best day of her life, but she had secretly been relieved.

Then a month before the wedding she found herself stuck with Mark in a pub on her own; she wasn't happy. Firstly, Em hated pubs unless they were her favourite kind – *pubs with no atmosphere*. In fact, Em's standard refrain whenever someone was foolish enough to ask where she wanted to go out that night was, without exception, '*A pub with no atmosphere*'. For Em *a pub with no atmosphere* was the perfect location for a great night out; no one else was there; you got served straight away; you got a seat and, if your luck was really in, no music was blaring in the background. What more could a middle-aged woman want on a night out? As you get older, you look at things differently. Only the other day Em had read in a newspaper that if you have two orgasms a week you live longer and she had immediately thought to herself, 'I'm on borrowed time'.

Secondly, not only was she in a pub with a hell of a lot of atmosphere, but she was stuck in it with Mark thanks to Alice and her Machiavellian attempts to try and engineer a friendship between the man in her life and her best friend. Alice laboured under the misapprehension that Mark and Em should get on, and if only Em spent more time with Mark, she would see the error of her ways.

Em had repeatedly tried to enlighten Alice that that particular trope in literature, TV and film where a woman hates a man and then by the end she grows to be enamoured with him was just that – a trope. It wasn't a reality: simply wishful thinking by presumably male scriptwriters/authors convinced that the reason they were unsuccessful with women wasn't down to their questionable personality but rather due to a lack of perspicacity by the women in their life.

'If you only got to know him better,' Alice would protest.

'I don't want to know him better. He's a bell end.'

'He isn't a bell end, Em. By the way, can you please stop saying that. It's not nice to hear him insulted like that.'

'It's hardly an insult. If you are going to object to me calling him a bell end then surely it can only be on the grounds that I'm stating the obvious. In my defence, he *is* a bell end.'

'He's not. He's very intelligent, very well-read, very sensitive.'

Em, who would be the first to admit she was extremely intelligent, extremely well-read and never one to be accused of false modesty, rejected this appraisal by Alice of her boyfriend's attributes.

'He might have read a lot of books but that doesn't mean he's bright. He is still a bell end.'

Alice was beginning to get angry now. Em could tell because Alice was getting into a strop and started to lecture Em on her lack of tolerance (true), her impatience (true) and that she was a bad judge of character (sometimes true but Em was convinced that in Mark she had hit the nail squarely on the head). Em half listened as she did what she always did when someone was having a go at her (her boss at work included), she thought about something else while rolling her eyes every now and then to give the impression that she was taking in what was being said but not liking it very much.

Alice was nothing if not persistent. True to form, she had arranged to meet Em in the rather appropriately named pub The Bell and then had texted Em just after they were supposed to meet up to say she was running late but Mark would see her in there. Alice's timing had been spot on. Em might not wish to see Mark but there was no way she was going to leave now, having just bought a drink, and then leave it unfinished. Em's only hope was to drink up quickly and hopefully be gone before Mark arrived. Unfortunately for Em, as she turned round to look for a seat in the packed pub, she spotted Mark waving at her. She was tempted to pretend she hadn't seen him but on the plus side he seemed to have managed to scrounge a corner table with two spare seats.

'Shit,' Em said out loud and clomped over to the table.

'Just got a text from Alice,' Mark explained. 'She thinks it would be good for us to get to know each other better. She said she would join us later.'

'I don't think it's necessary, do you? Shall we just drink up and go? I'm *her* friend after all. I don't need to be yours too.'

'I think I know what the problem is,' Mark said in his most patronising tone possible as he gestured in the air while Em rolled her eyes. Em suspected he'd been in the pub for a while and was already drunk.

'Well, I think the main problem is you're a bell end.'

'We all know you don't really think that.'

'Feel free to call a few of my mates to ask for confirmation,' Em replied. 'I even have the texts on my phone still.'

'Texts? What are you on about? Anyway, I think the real problem is that deep down you fancy me.'

Em was thunderstruck, confused as to whether Mark was just plain stupid (she already had her suspicions on that account) or he really didn't understand her at all.

This wasn't the first time Em had been faced with this kind of cod psychology. In her days as a would-be actor, decades ago, she had played Titania in a badly received production of A Midsummer's Night Dream. She had soon realised that the actor playing Oberon was an utter bell end. The actor playing Hermia, however, despite all evidence to the contrary, had been convinced Em's hatred for her fellow actor was due to her being in denial of her true feelings and that Em was secretly in love with him. She really wasn't. Em couldn't stand him, but try as she might, she was unable to convince her colleague otherwise. Decades later, Em was once more forced to state the obvious.

'I don't think that's the problem. I think you're a bell end. Believe me on that.'

'You're very rude, you know.'

'Well. I prefer to call it forthright. By the way, if you don't want to be called a bell end, stop acting like one. Stop belittling my mate, continuously finding fault with what she does, how she dresses and who she is and for fuck's sake stop telling her what she should and shouldn't read. Out of interest, does all that really make you feel better about yourself? Stop doing all that, and then you know what? I might stop calling you a bell end.'

'I don't know who you think you're kidding but we all know it's an act. Even Alice suspects you fancy me.'

At this Em almost choked on her drink. She appreciated love made you blind but could it really make you that dumb. Meanwhile Mark, seething at what he felt to be Em's pathetic denials, squeezed past the table and stood in front of Em, blocking her in as she sat perched on a high bar chair, backed up against the wall. It didn't take long for Em to realise she was cornered with no way out; surrounded by a cacophony of sound, in a packed pub with everyone busy minding their own business. Well, almost everyone.

'Is this guy bothering you, love?' A middle-aged man in a sharp suit, standing at the next table had placed himself behind Mark. The man was obviously out for a drink after a day in the office. Of average height and build, he was evidently prepared to stand his ground. His self-assurance was aided and abetted somewhat by the fact that the man he was with loomed even larger and manifestly spent a lot of time in the gym. Mark turned round and was about to say something until he spotted the man's friend.

'We're having a bit of a tête-à-tête,' Mark explained.

'He *is* bothering me,' Em replied. She appreciated that if she were a character in a recent film then she would be some kind of kick-ass feminist ninja who could Kung Fu the hell out of Mark but this was real life and if these two guys could get rid of him for her so much the better.

'I think you should leave,' the man in the sharp suit said, 'don't you?'

Mark was about to say something when the guy's friend repeated the question. Mark huffed, grabbed his drink, finished it off in one go and swiftly left the pub.

'Thanks,' Em said.

'You're welcome,' the man in the sharp suit replied. 'Would you like a drink?'

'I could do with one,' Em replied and all three laughed.

Forty minutes later the *looming large man* had left, leaving Em and her knight in shining armour to their own devices. Against all the odds - her saviour was in banking - Em was enjoying his company. She didn't even mind she was in a pub with atmosphere for once. She switched her phone to silent to better ignore the now constant calls from Alice as she and *sharp suit man* made themselves heard over the noise in the bar.

A month later, Em unexpectedly had a plus one for Alice's wedding. She had thought it a bit premature to ask *sharp suit man*, as she tended to refer to her latest love interest with her mates, but he had suggested coming along and Em, relieved not to be stuck on the singles table yet again, had agreed. Luckily for Em, Alice had a tender heart and had forgiven her for her outburst with Mark in the pub on the strict proviso that Em was banned from saying the word bell end on the day of her wedding. Em had reluctantly agreed and even she had to admit that Alice and Mark made a lovely-looking couple, even though she was still convinced Alice was making the biggest mistake of her life.

Later that evening, sitting at a table for 'couples', *sharp suit man* was being interrogated by all and sundry. Rarely was Em an item with anyone and her appearance with a beau had almost been in danger of upstaging the happy couple. For once, Em took a backseat as *sharp suit* man answered numerous questions about his past life – never been married, no kids, lived in Tooting, two brothers, one sister, voted remain, no pets, aged 52, didn't smoke and his favourite film was Star Wars. It was only then Em realised that in the whole month of seeing him she had never asked half of these questions herself.

'Did you always want to be a banker?' Jeanette asked, a good friend of both Em and Alice. It seemed a most unlikely possibility, but Jeanette was nothing if not naïve.

'Oh, no. When I was young, I always wanted to be an actor. The next Harrison Ford,' *sharp suit man* replied.

Everyone laughed at that. *Sharp suit man* wasn't bad looking but he looked nothing like Harrison Ford in his prime.

'I can see that,' Jeanette replied with a simper. It had to be said Jeanette was a terrible flirt. 'Did you ever do any acting?'

'I gave it a go, years ago but it just wasn't for me: the insecurity, the rejection, the nutters you have to work with. I was a right Bohemian back then. Long hair, long beard, horn-rimmed glasses with a penchant for silver jewellery and second-hand clothes.'

'A rather different look from the one you're sporting now,' Jeanette pointed out while twirling the end of a lock of hair round a finger. 'Why did you stop?'

'I suppose the final straw was when I was playing Oberon in a production of A Midsummer's Night Dream. Oh, the harridan I had to work with as Titania. Rude, inconsiderate, self-righteous, you wouldn't believe what a bitch she was to work with. She made my life a living nightmare. I had such a horrendous time with her it put me off acting for life. Imagine that. I'd always wanted to be an actor. It was my dream for as long as I could remember. Then I work six weeks with that bitch and I never want to act again.'

Sharp suit man chuckled at the thought of what had been six of the worst weeks of his life, then he turned to Em with a wink.

Dying with Laughter

'Morag,' her mother shouted, the harsh consonants of her East coast Scottish accent ricocheting around the dingy room. 'This woman is claiming she doesn't have to pay.'

Morag turned round from flirting with Evan, one of a batch of new male stand up comedians with floppy hair who insisted on wearing remarkably tight trousers. Evan wasn't that good a comedian. His current five minute set consisted of him noticing a lot of stuff. Sadly, the one thing he had failed to notice in its entirety were the punchlines missing from his jokes. Endowed, as he was, with such a lack of comedic potential, Morag would normally have ignored him, but she was willing to make an exception. In other words, Evan was young and strikingly handsome, and Morag was deluded enough to believe she was in with a chance, despite being old enough to be his mother. Technically, she was *older* than Evan's mother but, fortunately for Morag, she was in a blissful state of ignorance on that score. Morag's eyes swept up to the woman who had the temerity to try and get past her mum without paying and let out a heartfelt sigh.

'She'd be right, mum. She doesn't have to pay.'

'Why's that, may I ask?'

Her mother's sharp tones reverberated around the room. If anything, her anger had intensified.

'That's Jackie Owens, mum. She's a comedian. She's the headline act.'

'Well, how was I supposed to know that?'

Before Morag had a chance to reply, Jackie reminded Ina that she had mentioned all this when she had tried to get in. Several times. Ina was unabashed. Not one for admitting she was in the wrong, even when she was, Ina countered with what she deemed a justifiable excuse.

'Yes, but anyone can say that, can't they?'

Realising that her mum was still blocking Jackie's entrance into the small basement room that was home to her regular new material comedy night in the depths of North London, Morag approached her mum and pointed to the poster on the wall next to her.

'Mum, the main clue is that Jackie's face is on the poster. In fact, besides mine, it's the only face on the poster.'

'Not forgetting,' Jackie added through gritted teeth, 'we've met several times before. I'm Morag's best friend. Remember, Mrs MacLeod. You've been to my flat.'

'Have I?'

'Yes. Several times.'

'You look different.'

Ina MacLeod put on her specs as if to confirm the accuracy of her latest statement as she scrutinised Jackie from head to foot. For her part, Jackie couldn't help wondering how Ina could possibly see anything through them, given how smeared with grease the lenses were.

'Well, to give mum her due, Jackie,' Morag said, in an attempt to placate her mother who took any loss of revenue at the box office as a personal affront, 'you have had your hair cut rather short recently.'

'I've had a trim,' Jackie countered in a much louder voice than she had intended, but she was becoming narked. She was the wronged party after all and she wasn't quite sure how she had ended up having to defend herself.

'A trim? That's some trim. Talk about your hair being on the short side. If you ask me, it makes you look like a bloke.'

Jackie sighed in exasperation, but decided to make a joke out of it.

'How many times do I have to tell you, Mrs MacLeod? I'm not a bloke. I'm a lesbian.'

Morag decided to use a diversionary tactic on her mother that she had used with great success many times before.

'Mum, do you want to get back to the door,' she whispered. 'I think that posh English guy is trying to sneak in.'

'The English …..' Ina immediately directed her ire towards the man next in line who happened to be Portuguese, newly arrived in the UK, and had no idea what Ina was saying to him or why she seemed so angry about it all.

'That always does the trick,' Morag said, ushering Jackie into the sound booth which also served as storage cupboard and green room.

'What does what?' Jackie asked, as she looked for a space to plonk down her capacious rucksack.

'I only have to mention "posh English person" and my mum is off on the war path.'

'If she's that anti-English, why does she live in England? Why not go back to Scotland?'

'Look, my mum might have been in London since the 1960s, but she's still incredibly patriotic. She would do anything for Scotland. I mean ANYTHING. Anything that is apart from go back and live there.'

'I see. Mind you, I see why you get your mum to do the door for you. No one gets past her in a hurry. I don't want to sound big-headed, but my face was on the poster that was stuck on the wall right next to her.'

'And on the flyers,' Morag added.

'Brilliant. Not only am I not recognised from off the telly, primarily because I never get asked to go on there in the first place, but I'm not even recognised from the publicity I am on!'

'It is quite an old photo,' Morag trailed off, and then brightened. 'Things could be worse.'

Jackie might be joking but Morag knew it was a sore point for her best friend that her career hadn't taken the trajectory she had imagined it would and which, by rights, she deserved.

'Things *are* a lot worse. My brother just texted me.'

'Your brother?' Morag sounded unusually animated and started searching for her make up bag within the depths of her cavernous handbag.

'Yes, I got the text while I was on the way here. He wanted to warn me that my mum is in the audience as some kind of surprise.'

'Oh,' Morag sounded a lot less animated than she had been just seconds before and immediately called off the search for her make up.

Jackie noted that Morag did not seem surprised by the news of her mother's imminent appearance. If anything, Morag looked somewhat guilty as well as strangely disappointed.

'Your mum is already here,' she explained. 'She brought us in bags of food earlier, just in case we got hungry.'

Morag pointed to two carrier bags down by the sound desk, both packed full of food. On the chair next to them lay two discarded crisp packets and an empty box of chocolate fingers.

'This is for the two of us?'

'Don't be daft! These are my bags. Your ones are over there.'

Morag pointed to another two carrier bags, replete with what looked like fruit, standing by the door. Jackie was about to question the marked difference in the bags' contents, suspecting there had been some avid re-divvying by Morag before she'd arrived, but Morag beat her to the punch.

'Oh yes, just so you know, that's not the only thing she's brought with her.'

'What do you mean? Not more food?'

'No. I think she's brought a date with her.'

Jackie burst out into uncontrollable laughter, tripping over her rucksack in the process.

'What are you on about? My mum hasn't been on a date for the last 30 years.'

'Well, she's with some guy tonight.'

'Are you sure he's with her as in *with her*?'

'I think so. He looks terrified. Before I forget, did you hear what happened to Jim Jacks?'

Jackie groaned. Just hearing that name reminded Jackie of her numerous years as an open spot, doing dire gigs, playing to no one but other comics, and slowly losing the will to live.

'Don't tell me he is still going? He was an open spot when I first started 20 years ago. Surely, he should have taken the hint by now and packed it in.'

Even as she said it, Jackie suspected the worst. It was amazing the delusion that clouded some people's judgement. You would think standing on stage year in year out to minimal laughter and perennially faced with a dearth of gig offers would be a big enough hint that maybe comedy wasn't for you, but for the likes of Jimmy Jacks it evidently wasn't.

As for Morag, she was thrilled; she had hot comedy news for once that Jackie knew nothing about. That was a rare occurrence in itself and this news was mega. Morag sidled up to Jackie, looked around in case someone had somehow magically managed to sneak into the sound booth without either of them noticing and whispered into Jackie's ear for a more dramatic effect.

'Jim Jacks died last night.'

'That's it. That's the gossip. Jim Jacks died,' Jackie replied, every word dripping in sarcasm. 'He always dies. He's died ever since he started stand up 25 years ago. When has he ever NOT died? That's hardly news, Morag.'

'No, dies as in dies.'

'What are you on about? I told you, Morag. Jim Jacks dying is not news.'

'No, not dies, DIES.'

'What?'

'Dies, as in kick the bucket, dies.'

The enormity of what Morag had been trying to tell her finally sunk in.

'When? How?' Jackie asked.

'Last night. At a new material night in Penge. Rumour has it he was murdered.'

'Well, South London can be a tough crowd. How bad did he do exactly?'

'Very funny. Well, I presume he must have annoyed somebody. Who do you think it could be?'

'Anyone who had the misfortune of watching his act, I should imagine. I'm guessing police have narrowed down possible suspects to a mere five thousand disappointed comedy fans. Let alone all the poor comics who had to follow him.'

With a comedian's wont to turn any situation to being about them, Jackie was about to launch into a story about one of the times she'd gigged with Jim, when the door to the sound booth opened. Both women looked round as Jackie's mum, Pilar, marched purposefully into the room. Given the cramped nature of the sound booth, it was an impressive feat to pull off.

'So, you're here at last. Morag has been here for ages,' Pilar said with an accent unmistakably that of a pissed off Spanish woman.

'She would be, mum. She runs the night.'

'Did you get the food? I put together a few bits and pieces.'

'Yes, mum. Morag did mention you brought a few things in. Talking of bringing things. What's this about you being on a date?'

'Oh Tim. It was your brother's idea. Oh my God. He's so boring, Jackie.'

'I don't think Jackie's brother is that boring, Pilar. I know he's an accountant and all that, but someone has to be,' said Morag who had a soft spot for Jackie's older brother.

'No, I don't mean my own son,' Pilar's voice rose a few notches in irritation. 'I mean Tim. The man is tedious. Tedious. Maybe I could introduce him to you, Morag? You're always single.'

'You're all right, Pilar. Thanks.'

'So why are you out on a date with him if he's so boring?' Jackie asked.

'You know, I would love to be a lesbian like you Jackie. Thing is I like co...'

Never in their lives had Morag and Jackie been so happy for Morag's phone to start ringing.

'Thank Christ for that,' Jackie muttered under her breath.

Morag grabbed the opportunity to leave Pilar and Jackie alone and exited the sound booth to take the call, but was stopped in her tracks by yet another kerfuffle surrounding her mum.

'That's £5. Each,' Ina snarled.

'Madam, as I've explained to you several times already. My name is Detective Inspector MacKay,' said a stocky man in a trench coat, who was ill-advisedly waving his warrant card in front of Ina's nose. 'We are the police and this is a murder enquiry. We don't need to buy tickets. Will you kindly let us in?'

'As I've explained to you, no one is getting past me without paying.'

'Doyle. Arrest her for obstruction.'

'Just try it. The only way you're getting me out of here is in a box.'

'Maybe we should just pay the £5, sir,' Detective Sergeant Doyle interjected. A mild mannered man, slight of build, with receding hair and horn glasses, he seemed remarkably ill-built as a bastion of law and order. 'Couldn't we claim it against expenses?'

Morag felt sorry for him, particularly as DI MacKay didn't seem that elated at this suggestion. The call would have to wait. She switched off the phone and walked up to the desk.

'For goodness sake, mum. Let them in.'

'Why? They're not on the poster. Though they do look like a bunch of clowns.'

'MUM! Look, please come in, Inspector. Shall we go into the sound booth?'

Morag was keen to be helpful but instantly regretted her decision on entering the sound booth. She'd forgotten how small the booth was. It was getting very cramped and it looked as if she had interrupted Jackie and Pilar in mid-argument.

'Who are they?' Pilar asked, annoyed at being interrupted midway through berating her daughter for her latest haircut.

'Christ, not another one. Saga Special Ops are out in force tonight,' DI MacKay whispered to DS Doyle.

'It's the police, Pilar,' Morag explained as she squeezed past the collection of bodies at the door.

'Jackie, what have you done?' Pilar asked and stepped towards her daughter.

'No, no. It's nothing to do with Jackie,' Morag interjected. 'I presume it's because Jim Jacks died last night. Is that right, officer?'

'Who?' Pilar asked.

'You wouldn't know him, mum,' Jackie explained.

'No, she does,' Morag replied. 'Remember when we did that club off The Strand years back. He was doing a short spot and Pilar stood up and screamed at him to get off, half way through his set.'

'Oh yes. How could I forget? What a wonderful evening that was,' Jackie agreed in full sarcasm mode.

'Oh, him. I remember. He was awful.' Pilar looked as if she still bore a grudge.

'Well, he died last night, Pilar,' Morag explained.

'But he must always die. So what? Who are they? The comedy police.'

'No, he's died as in dies, dies,' Morag explained.

'That's what I said. He always dies. Why are the police here? That's not a crime. If it was, you two would have been arrested years ago,' Pilar replied.

Morag was about to say something in hers and Jackie's defence, but decided against it. After all, Pilar had attended many a gig when she and Jackie had first started out in comedy and she had witnessed many a comedy death by both of them over the years.

'No, dies, dies. As in kick the bucket, dies,' Morag explained in an attempt to revert the conversation back to its original subject.

'You seem very knowledgeable, madam,' DI MacKay noted. 'Were you there last night?'

'At a new material night in Penge? How badly do you think my career is going?' Morag sounded affronted.

'Would we have seen you on the telly?' DS Doyle asked, peering over the shoulder of DI MacKay who seemed aggrieved at his underling's sudden intervention.

'No,' Morag said, smiling to hide her frustration at being asked that particular question for the umpteenth time in her career, 'I'm more of a club comic.'

'What does that mean?' DI MacKay asked.

'I'm funny.'

'You know what you should do,' DS Doyle said, warming to the theme.

'What's that?' Morag asked despite herself.

'Go on Live at the Apollo.'

'You don't say?' Morag replied as Jackie mimed bashing her head against the wall in solidarity at Morag having to listen to such stupidity.

'I never thought of that. Thanks for the tip. I'll give them a ring tomorrow.'

Morag worried for a second if her sarcasm had gone a bit too far. He was a policeman after all. She then realised that DS Doyle thought she was deadly serious. Morag sighed and glanced at Jackie for some much needed moral support.

'Anyway, to answer your question,' Morag said in an attempt to forestall any more ludicrous advice, 'I wasn't there last night. I happened to see a link on Facebook to Pat Stevens' blog about it. It was all on there including the fact that the police were questioning everyone. According to Pat's blog they were there for ages.'

'Yes, I'm afraid so. There were a lot of people to process.'

'At a new material night?' Jackie and Morag asked in unison. They were both thinking the same thing: a lot of people at a new material night? In Penge of all places? That didn't sound right at all.

'Yes,' DI MacKay confirmed, quickly looking at his notes, 'there were 23 comics, 2 audience members and some tramp asleep at the back of the room.'

'Ahh,' Jackie and Morag both replied, relieved that the mystery of a well-attended new material night had been suitably explained.

'Who was the tramp?' Pilar asked.

'Probably the promoter,' Jackie suggested.

'Or a reviewer?' Morag countered.

'Snack anyone? Home-made,' Pilar said, proffering a big Tupperware box around the booth. It had been at least 10 minutes and no one had eaten anything so she felt that was the least she could do.

'Not now, madam. Thank you,' DI MacKay replied as he smacked away DS Doyle's out-stretched arm reaching past him to the food on offer. 'Talking of Pat Stevens, we have reason to believe he's here. Would you be able to point him out to us? Out of interest, how long do we have before the show starts? I thought it started at 8. It's 8:05 now. I was worried it might have already started. I did note there was someone on stage when we were trying to get past your mother.'

'Oh, no. It's a comedy show. So, we say we start at 8 but it's 8ish. So probably in another 5 minutes.'

'Then why, may I ask, was someone on stage? Is that usual?' DI MacKay asked.

'Oh, that'll be Rich. He's a bit precious. He always wants to test out the mic beforehand. If the mic is not just right, he gets in a right state. It's either allow him to play with the mic before the show or have him send me a bloody long email afterwards wanging on about how the mic somehow adversely affected how well his jokes went down.'

'Can a mic do that?' DS Doyle asked, peering once more around the solid frame of DI MacKay.

'Not as much as falling out with the guy who writes your best material,' Jackie replied, and gave Morag a knowing look.

'If we can get to the matter at hand, ladies. I should introduce myself. I am Detective Inspector MacKay and this is Detective Sergeant Doyle. And you are?'

'Morag MacLeod. The compere.'

'So, you're not a comic then?' DI MacKay asked.

'Yes, I am a comic,' Morag explained as if to a foreigner who had committed the cardinal sin of not speaking fluent English.

'But you said just now you were the compere,' DI MacKay looked down at his notes as if to confirm what had just been said.

Morag and Jackie again exchanged looks.

'Yes, I think you'll find that a compere at a comedy night is also a comic,' Morag explained as if to a young child, a foreign one, who too had committed the cardinal sin of not having English as his mother tongue.

'I think DI MacKay means you're not a proper comic, are you? I presume that once you get good enough, are you hoping to become a proper comic?' DS Doyle asked. He sounded genuinely interested.

'A compere IS a proper comic I think you'll find,' Morag replied through pursed lips.

'Is Morag a stage name?' DI MacKay asked in an attempt to move the conversation forward.

'Yes, I decided to call myself Morag to add a bit of glamour to the act.'

'Really?' DS Doyle interjected.

'No!' It was Jackie's turn to roll her eyes in support of her friend.

The door to the booth opened, forcing DS Doyle to step onto the bags of food. He was mumbling his apologies as Chantelle Harris sashayed into the room. In her early twenties, Chantelle was tall and thin with deep-blue eyes and long blonde hair. She was stunningly attractive, dressed in shorts and a t-shirt which left little to the imagination. She looked round the room, flashing her deep-blue eyes and wide smile.

'Hi Morag. Sorry to interrupt. I was wondering if I could squeeze on tonight.'

'Sorry, Chantelle. As I told you on the phone and by email and by text, and in reply to your several WhatsApp and Facebook messages, no can do. We're full up.'

'I just thought you could...'

'NO!' Morag replied, channelling her best imitation of her mother in a bad mood.

Morag had assumed this would ensure that Chantelle would beat a hasty retreat, but Chantelle was nothing if not pushy, and she went to sit down on one of the chairs.

'Sorry, if you don't mind, Miss. We're in the middle of something,' DI MacKay explained in a tone of voice which left very little wriggle room.

For a second, Chantelle looked as if she was still intent on standing her ground, but then evidently thought better of it. She turned on her heels and smiled alluringly at DI MacKay.

'Of course. Sorry to disturb,' and with a final flourish of a smile Chantelle sashayed back out of the sound booth.

'Good God,' Pilar snarled.

'She is?' DS Doyle inquired. He had become somewhat animated by Chantelle's appearance. It didn't go unnoticed by DI MacKay who turned round to look at him with obvious disdain.

'Chantelle Harris,' Morag explained. 'A relatively new comic. Mind you, she's done two full-length Edinburgh shows, yet is still to write one decent joke.'

'She's attractive for a female comic, don't you think?' DS Doyle asked.

'Thanks,' Morag replied.

'No, it's just that I thought female comics tended to be... You know what I mean. Take you, for example, you're more in the traditional vein of female comedians, ... overweight, um.... What I meant to say, your colleague Jackie here, is, I would say, more conventionally attractive.'

'And nevertheless funny,' Jackie added who didn't appear to take DS Doyle's take on her looks as much of a compliment.

'Yes, but you're a lesbian,' Morag pointed out. 'And as we know, women can only be funny if they are either overweight…..'

'A lesbian…' Jackie interjected.

'Or Jewish.'

'Is that right?' DS Doyle asked.

DS Doyle sounded fascinated by this theory. Morag and Jackie both sighed. Both women had been in the business for years and were sick to death of being asked by some hack of a radio producer or journalist to comment on the spurious contention that women weren't funny. Perhaps even more annoying were the ludicrous theories used to explain away why such and such a female comedian was funny and an exception to the rule: theories which all had one thing in common. They were never empirical, but based on sheer blind prejudice. Morag and Jackie appreciated they could explain all this but what would be the point? Instinctively, they both opted for the much shorter version of an explanation, and shouted: 'No!'

'Chantelle is single, Sergeant, if you're wondering,' Jackie informed him.

DS Doyle's ears pricked up at the news and, in his excitement, he finally freed his left foot from the confines of one of the plastic bags.

'Really?' he asked.

'She's a female comic. Of course, she's single,' Morag explained.

'That surprises me,' DS Doyle said with a quizzical look on his face. 'It's such a male-dominated industry I would have thought…'

'That someone that attractive would be inundated with offers,' Morag interrupted. 'Well, the thing is, officer, she's so annoying that male comics avoid her. Have you any idea how annoying an attractive, blond woman in their early 20s has to be for male comics to give her a pass?'

'She's that annoying?' DS Doyle asked. He looked crestfallen at the thought.

'Any chance we could get back to the investigation?' DI MacKay demanded impatiently, his attempt to get everyone's attention was completely ignored by Pilar who was getting seriously worried that no one had eaten for quite some time.

'Sausage roll, anyone?' she asked.

'Oh, yes, please, Pilar,' Morag replied. Never one to miss out on food, Morag was only surprised she hadn't noticed them before now.

'Madam,' DI MacKay screeched. He was beginning to lose his patience. 'Could you forget the catering for a second? This is a murder enquiry.'

'I know. But people still have to eat.'

'Inspector,' Morag said as she motioned her finger towards the sound booth's window. 'You mentioned you wanted to talk to Pat Stevens earlier. He's the guy talking to Chantelle at the back of the room, if you still need to speak to him.'

Everyone stared at the man Morag was pointing at. Middle aged, obese, dressed in faded jeans and a moth-eaten jumper he was in an animated conversation with Chantelle who was smiling up at him adoringly. They watched in silence for several seconds as Chantelle flirted with him.

'Pat Stevens is a comedian?' DI MacKay asked, finally breaking the silence.

'God, no,' Jackie replied. 'He was but he was awful. No comedy bones whatsoever. So now he reviews comedy on that damn blog of his.'

'Doyle, can you bring him into the sound booth? I'd like to have a word with our Mr Stevens.'

Pilar used the opportunity to hand out more snacks, much to the disdain of DI MacKay, while Morag attempted to create more room in the booth by stuffing various bags under the sound desk. She tried to pick up Jackie's rucksack, almost gave herself a hernia and thought better of it.

'What the hell have you got in here?' she asked.

Before Jackie could reply the door to the booth opened and Pat walked in, his eyes darting around the room as they moved from person to person.

'I understand you are a comedy reviewer, Mr Stevens,' DI MacKay said, forcing Pat Stevens' attention to rest solely on him.

'Yes, that's correct.'

'Do you need any special training for that?'

'Well, I did do a two week intensive comedy course a few years back.'

Jackie and Morag groaned in the background.

'I see. Am I correct in thinking, Mr Stevens, in your capacity as a reviewer, you were at yesterday's gig where Jim Jacks died?'

'Yes. Yes, I was. Would you mind, Inspector, if I filmed our chat? I'd love to stick this on my blog.'

Pat took his phone out of his pocket and waved it in front of the Inspector. One of the many faults that Pat had as a would-be comic was his inability to read a room. Now no longer a comedian, this skill was evidently still lacking.

'Doyle,' DI MacKay said, shooting Pat a withering glance, 'could you relieve Mr Stevens of his phone, please? Does that answer your question?'

DS Doyle stepped forward. For a second Pat contemplated resisting DI MacKay's request. The inspector shot him another withering glance and Pat handed over his most prized possession.

'You'll get it back once we've finished, Mr Stevens,' DI MacKay reassured him. 'So, as the only person here who was at last night's murder scene, I'd...'

'No. I wasn't,' Pat replied.

'Sorry? You weren't what?'

'I'm not the only person here who was also at last night's murder scene. Chantelle popped in for a bit to try out new stuff. And that tramp was there too.'

'The tramp?'

'Yes, but it's odd. She's dressed the same but she's doing the door here tonight.'

***

Everyone looked at Morag who was staring at the sound desk as if she had dropped a contact lens among all the knobs and faders. The silence continued so Morag decided to peer through the misted-up window of the sound booth instead.

'That *is* odd,' Morag finally said.

'What, that someone mistook your mum for a tramp?' Jackie asked. Jackie didn't sound that surprised.

'No, not that. Rich doesn't seem to be on stage any more, and I can't see him in the room. Where the hell has he gone? Given the state of most of the other acts we need a strong opener.'

Jackie squeezed past her mum and joined Morag in staring out of the window.

'And why is everyone standing up and staring at the stage. He hasn't got his cock out again.'

'Well, there's no chance of making that out from here,' Morag noted without the least touch of irony.

While Pilar barged towards them to get a better look, there was a kerfuffle at the door as Pilar's date, a tall, bespectacled man in his early sixties, with short grey hair attempted to squeeze past DS Doyle and DI MacKay.

'Sorry to bother you, but I think that comic has just died on stage.'

'Don't be daft,' Jackie said, 'he won the Perrier back in the '90s. Anyway, he was just trying out the mic. The show hasn't started yet.'

'No,' the man explained, looking embarrassed at having to explain further. 'He's died, died. As in kick the bucket, died.'

'Oh, bloody hell,' Morag exclaimed. She seemed genuinely upset.

'I didn't know you two were that close friends,' Jackie said at the look of unexpected anguish in Morag's face.

'No, it's not that,' Morag replied. 'I'll have to give people their money back. Try explaining that to my mum.'

***

Everyone except Pat had been ushered out of the sound booth by the police and had gone to sit at the far end of the room, their view of the stage marred by a massive stone pillar. Morag and Jackie had instinctively chosen this spot to be as far away as possible from both the public and the other comics. All you could hear in the eerie silence was the occasional refrain of Ina in shouty mode as she explained for the umpteenth time, 'How many times do I have to say it? No one is getting a refund.'

'Don't get upset, Morag, about tonight,' Jackie said, trying to reassure her best friend. 'I know this night has gone tits up, but with a bit of luck, you never know, you might get an Edinburgh show out of it.'

In times of trouble, it was the best form of consolation a comic could ever give to a fellow comedian.

'Who is that person?' Pilar asked, pointing to a woman in white PPE who was standing by the stage.

'I think it's forensics, mum.'

'Should I ask if they would like something to eat? It seems a bit rude.'

'I'd let her finish what she's doing first.'

'Should we still be here?' Pilar's date pointed out. He was clutching at straws in his desperation to leave. He was sure Pilar was a lovely woman, but she scared the living daylights out of him and in a previous life he'd done two tours in Afghanistan.

'Well, they did tell us to wait,' Morag replied. She was damned if she was going to miss out on this juicy gossip.

'I'm not sure they'll be impressed with us having what is to all intents and purposes a mini picnic at the back of the room,' Pilar's date said.

'That's Tim all over. You are so boring,' Pilar informed him. 'Oh, my God. A person has to eat. Here, you're English. Take a Scotch egg.'

'What?' Ina roared. Although she was sitting on the other side of the room, Ina had remarkably good hearing when it came to anyone besmirching her native country's honour.

'Mum. Leave it!' Morag called over. Dropping her voice to a stage whisper she turned to Jackie. 'Look, that idiot Pat Stevens is coming out the booth already. He wasn't in there for that long. Given the way he waffles that's an achievement in itself.'

'Yes, but that Doyle doesn't look happy,' Jackie noted.

Pat shuffled towards them and sat down.

'Scotch egg?' Pilar asked.

No sooner had Pat joined them, Chantelle sashayed her way over.

'Do you mind if I join you?' she asked.

'Yes,' Morag and Jackie replied. As half expected, Chantelle ignored them.

'I was wondering now Rich is dead there's presumably a gap going. I'm available...'

'Not now, thanks,' Morag answered.

'I can easily..'

'As I said, not now.'

'Oh, OK. It's just….'

'Chantelle,' Pat intervened, 'do you want to pull up a chair and sit next to me? I'd love to interview you some time about your career.'

'That'll be a short article,' Jackie mouthed to Morag who laughed in agreement.

'Jesus wept,' Pilar muttered under her breath and opened up another Tupperware box.

Meanwhile raised voices could be heard from within the booth.

'For the fifth time, Doyle, will you go and fetch that woman in for questioning.'

'Can we not interview the young comic first?' DS Doyle's plaintive request vibrated through the sound booth window which Morag had purposefully left slightly ajar in the hope she could still hear what was going on.

'I think it's more pertinent to talk to the older woman, don't you?'

'Any chance of back up?' DS Doyle sounded scared.

'Doyle. She's an old age pensioner. You're a highly trained police officer.'

'I know, Sir. But she's really scary.'

'Oh, for goodness' sake, I'll go and fetch her myself.'

DI MacKay marched past his subordinate and in a couple of strides faced the picnic party.

'What the hell is going on here?'

'Tell me about it. Those two are flirting. Badly.' Pilar pointed to Pat and Chantelle. 'And we're having some food. Scotch egg?'

'I can see that, Madam. It's like a picnic in here. Where the hell did you get the tablecloth from?'

'Yes, but we are about three metres away from the body. So, what's the big deal?' Pilar replied, while opening up yet another piece of Tupperware.

'How much is three metres in English?' Morag asked. Having been taught imperial measurements one week at school and then metric the next, her concept of distance was sketchy at best.

'Presumably it's this far from the stage,' Jackie replied despite not being too sure how long three meters was either.

'But the body is still lying there, Madam,' DI MacKay replied.

'Well, it is face down,' Pilar explained with what to her was a self-evident end to any further argument.

'What difference does that make?' DI MacKay asked.

'You never saw what he looked like,' Ina shouted out across the room.

'While I am here, can you confirm that's Rich...' DI MacKay interjected.

'Rich Walker. Yes,' Jackie replied.

'What kind of mood was Mr Walker in, would you say? Happy, sad?'

'Well, he was a bit narked that he was opening,' Morag admitted. 'He felt he should be the one closing the gig not Jackie.'

'So, he was depressed, you'd say?'

'Not to the extent he'd commit suicide on stage, I don't think. No,' Morag reassured him.

Morag contemplated whether she should bother explaining to the inspector that there was a school of thought among some comics that it was a personal insult of the grossest magnitude if they didn't close the show. Morag had never subscribed to this belief. Personally, as long as it didn't mean losing out on extra money, Morag was of the persuasion that going on first and then being able to piss off home straight away afterwards was the ideal combination when it came to gigging. Morag was also toying with the idea of giving the inspector a quick retrospective of Rich's career when she saw from the corner of her eye, her mother thud across the room.

'What's the problem?' Ina asked. Sensing trouble, she had deserted her post, cash box in hand, ready to join in.

'Ah, Mrs MacLeod, just the person. I'd like a word with you, please.'

'You're not getting your money back. I don't care who you are.'

'They didn't pay, remember?' Morag reminded her.

'What?' Apparently, the simple act of being reminded that someone hadn't paid was enough to set Ina off again.

'We're the police, madam. As I have explained to you several times already. We don't have to pay.'

'That's extortion,' Ina pointed out.

'Madam, we are investigating a murder.'

'I only punched him,' Ina replied.

'Who?'

Morag thought it was prudent to mouth to her mother, 'Don't think he's talking about *that*, mum.'

'I have reason to believe Mrs MacLeod that you were at the Laughing Zebra last night in Penge. Is that correct? Well, Mrs MacLeod?'

'Yes, I was,' Ina admitted. 'What of it?'

DS Doyle, who had steeled himself to back up the inspector interjected.

'The inspector would like a word, Madam.'

DI MacKay turned to look at DS Doyle and with exasperation coating every syllable, informed him, 'I can handle this, thank you.'

***

As the sound of ambulance and police car sirens faded into the distance, Morag and Jackie finished picking up the contents of the cash box from off the floor.

'How's Detective Inspector MacKay?' Morag asked, as soon as DS Doyle returned to the room.

'I've been assured that it's only a slight concussion,' DS Doyle replied. 'He's been taken to hospital just to be on the safe side.'

'Tortilla?' Pilar asked in an attempt to break the tension.

'Your mum is deceptively strong for a woman of her age and build,' DS Doyle added as he helped himself to the proffered food.

'Tell me about it. Some guy tried to mug her recently.'

'What happened?'

'He ended up in hospital too by all accounts.'

'Good,' Pilar interjected.

'Didn't the police charge her?' Pat asked, wondering if he could somehow include this little titbit on his blog.

'You think some young punk is going to admit he was beaten up by an old age pensioner? And a woman at that?'

'You do recall I am the police? You've just confessed to your mum committing at the very minimum ABH.'

'She was exaggerating. You know for comedy purposes,' Jackie lied.

'Salad?' Pilar asked in yet another attempt to turn the conversation around.

'I'm surprised,' Pat asked, looking for an angle, 'that you didn't offer to go with your mum to the police station?'

'While she's in that mood. You have to be joking. I rang my dad instead. He can sort it. And if you think my mum is a walking Scottish cliché, wait till you meet him. At home, he plays Jimmy Shand on a loop. It was one of the reasons my mum was able to cite unreasonable behaviour in their divorce proceedings.'

'Jimmy who?' DS Doyle asked.

'Don't worry about it. Talk of the devil.'

'Jimmy Shand is here?' DS Doyle asked, looking round.

'No! Don't be daft. Jimmy Shand died years ago. I mean my dad. Hi, dad,' Morag shouted at the man walking through the door. Morag began waving her arm and stuck her head around the pillar so he could make her out all the more easily. Tall, with flowing white hair and a bushy white beard, he came across as a Scottish Captain Birds Eye.

'That was quick,' Morag noted.

'Well, it sounded urgent. What's your mum been up to now? Is she here still?'

'No, she's not. As I said, she's down at the nick. I told you to go there not here.'

'Oh, no. Ina is nothing to do with me anymore. I'm only here because of you. What exactly happened? I couldn't make out what you were saying on that mobile phone. You talk far too fast.'

While Morag was at a loss as to where to start, Morag's dad took the opportunity to stare at Jackie and ask her if she was a witness to what had happened.

'Well, she is kind of but this is Jackie who you've met before. Don't you remember her?'

'I think so. You look different from last time somehow.'

'I had a trim, OK.'

'I told you it was far too short,' Pilar opined.

'Folks, this is my dad, Ron. Dad, this is Detective Sergeant Doyle, Pat Stevens, and this is Jackie's mum, Pilar and her friend, sorry, I don't know your name.'

'His name is Tim,' Pilar explained, flashing a smile in Ron's direction while offering him a Tupperware box full of tortilla.

'I thought you told me your name was Nick,' Pat said, looking confused, as he turned to the man of the moment.

'No, it isn't. All right? I should know the name of my date, shouldn't I?' Pilar announced to everyone. 'But he's not really a date,' Pilar added as an aside to Ron.

'Well, my name does happen to be Nick,' Nick confirmed.

'Really? I thought it was Tim. Why did you not say anything when I told people you were called Tim?'

'Sorry. I thought you were saying this is him. Not this is Tim. It must be your accent.'

'What accent? I don't have an accent.' Pilar sounded most offended and ironically more Spanish than usual.

'Anyway, dad, as I mentioned to you on the phone, they've arrested mum.'

'Not again! What is she supposed to have done this time?'

'The police think she might be involved in a couple of murders. That's hardly likely, is it?'

'Murder. No, no, of course not. Not unless blunt force trauma was involved. It wasn't, was it?'

'I don't think so, no.'

'So why do they suspect your mother?'

'I'm afraid that tramp ... I mean your mother was at both crime scenes,' Pat explained with a knowing look.

'Pat, are you implying my mum could be mistaken for a tramp?'

'Well, your mum does have a unique dress sense,' Ron conceded. 'As for her hair, it's always been a bit on the wild side at the best of times.'

'Nevertheless, you're hardly likely to mistake her for a tramp, are you?' Morag insisted.

This question was met with universal silence, forcing Morag to rely on her best friend's support. 'Are you, Jackie?'

'Cup cake, Morag?' was Jackie's valiant attempt to change the subject. At times, Jackie was more like her mother than she cared to admit.

As Morag grabbed the cup cake, the woman in white PPE approached them.

'Sorry to interrupt. I'm Cath Jenkins. I'm from the forensics team. There are quite a few drinks in the green room. We need to establish which drink belongs to whom.'

'Mine would have been the staple drink of unsuccessful comics,' Morag stated, 'a cheap and cheerful glass of tap water. With a straw in it. To save on the lippy.'

'Whose is the bottle of rum we found in a plastic bag?' Cath Jenkins asked.

'I wondered where that had got to,' Pilar mused. 'Well? What do you expect me to do? The prices in here are ridiculous. Can I have it back?'

'Not right now I'm afraid. It looks as if Mr Walker may have been poisoned. Am I right in thinking he went on stage with a beer and a bottle of water. Is that usual?'

'It was part of his act. He had this set piece about pretending to drink water when he was in fact drinking beer.'

'It was a lot funnier than Morag is making it sound,' Jackie reassured them.

'He went on with both drinks is what you are saying?' Cath Jenkins asked.

'Yes, and did what he always did, he put both down on a table at the front before he took the mic out of the mic stand.'

'Yep, I saw him do that,' Pat agreed. 'But weirdly, I saw that tramp woman, I mean Morag's mother, swap the water bottle. I mean you couldn't miss it. She walked up bold as brass and swapped it. Rich even made a joke about it. He said the water bottle must have tried to sneak past her at the door without paying.'

'Interesting,' Cath Jenkins said, giving Morag the once over.

'Is it?' DS Doyle asked.

'Ever so slightly. We suspect the poison was in the water bottle.'

'Oh Jesus,' Morag and Ron said in unison.

***

'Cut,' said a clipped upper middle class English accent. The accent in question belonged to Daisy, a go-getting comedy producer who seemed compelled to shop exclusively at Zara.

'We're not finished yet,' Morag said, coming out of character with the utmost of ease. Not surprisingly given that the roles Jackie and she had written in their latest attempt at sit com stardom were their real selves to a tee. They had decided it would make playing them a hell of a lot easier.

'It's not very realistic, is it?' said Jonathan, in a mockney accent, dressed in jeans and a T-shirt with several tattoos on his arms and to complete the look a man bun and a goatee beard.

'It's a comedy. It's not supposed to be,' Jackie explained.

'We're not trying to do a Ken Loach here,' Morag elaborated. 'It's a sit com. It's funny. The audience will go with it.'

'Will they though? I think it would be much funnier if Jackie and Morag were a lot younger,' Daisy whispered, directing her statement solely to Jonathan.

'No, it's funnier if they are older. If they are both living with their mothers in their 40s that's a lot funnier than if they are in their 20s. It makes them more of a loser. Think Steptoe and Son.'

'What's that?' Daisy asked. Jonathan looked equally nonplussed.

'We would attract a much younger audience if we followed that paradigm,' Daisy remarked in an aside to Jonathan.

'Young people don't watch TV. People our age watch TV,' Jackie insisted.

'To be brutally honest, I'm not convinced if either of you are the right fit to play the leads,' Jonathan flashed them an awkward smile.

'What do you mean?' Jackie was beginning to get angry now. 'They fit us like a glove. They are us. They even have our names.'

'Are you sure about that?' Daisy asked.

'What? What that they have the same names as us? Pretty sure, yes,' Jackie replied. 'You do remember we wrote the parts in the first place. We know who these characters are. They ARE us.'

At this point the other actors at the reading thought it wise to busy themselves with their scripts.

'I'm thinking Sue Perkins,' said Daisy in another aside to Jonathan.

'Think that's instead of you,' Morag quipped to Jackie.

'What are you on about? She's *older* than me!'

'Is she?' everyone asked including all the other actors who for a second looked up from perusing their scripts.

'Yes, she is,' Jackie replied, unable to mask entirely the doubt she was beginning to feel on the subject.

'Then for the other role, maybe Dawn French?' Jonathan suggested.

'Great idea. Or Ruth Jones? Liza Tarbuck?' Daisy suggested back, grinning at her originality of thought.

'You're just naming overweight comedy actors now,' Morag stated through clenched teeth. 'Overweight doesn't mean we are interchangeable, you know.'

Daisy raised an eyebrow, ignored Morag and turned to Jonathan as if neither Morag nor Jackie were there.

'If we get Ruth, we could make her lot Welsh instead of Scottish. It's the same thing more or less.'

It was times like this that Morag wished she had brought her mother to the reading.

***

'Cut,' said Jared, the producer, whose daywear, despite him hailing from Crewe, was a bright pink kimono matched with a pair of snazzy leather brogues. In a previous tea break Morag and Jackie had discussed in the unisex toilets for a full two minutes whether such a sartorial choice fell under the rubric of cultural appropriation. Sadly, their conversation had come to a sudden halt when Jackie noticed a shot of pink silk and leather brogues under the door of one of the cubicles. She nudged Morag who took a full thirty seconds to realise that they were far from being alone in the toilets as they had previously thought.

'Don't you think your portrayal of the comedy producers is a bit far-fetched? Who is going to believe that a comedy producer doesn't know the first thing about comedy?' Jared asked.

Both women looked at each other and, as if by mutual consent, shouted, 'Cut.'

An Ordinary Day

That was the day I thought I was going to be raped and murdered.

It's strange how such an ordinary day can turn on a sixpence. You think there would be some kind of sign: an ear-splitting thunderstorm raging in the background; a premonition that something is not quite right; maybe a black cat meandering past you or an abandoned ladder standing on the pavement that you just had to walk under.

As it was, the weather was lovely: yet another gorgeous, sunny, Californian day in early February. No thunderstorms. No premonitions. No black cats had ambled past me: no ladders had stood in my path. I was enjoying the final stages of my round-the-world trip, having travelled first to Austria to see mates, from there to Australia, New Zealand, Fiji, Cook Islands, Tahiti and, last but not least, I had arrived in the good, old U.S. of A.

It was the 90s, and I was at a loose end, drifting from one unfulfilling job to another. With money in the bank for once, I headed one damp and dismal November afternoon to the STA travel agency near Victoria Station in central London and bought myself a round-the-world ticket. I told myself it was because I had always wanted to see the world. I didn't. What I wanted to see was yet another guy I was enamoured with and who I had enjoyed a very close relationship with but where, yet again, nothing had happened between us. Despite all proof to the contrary, I was convinced deep-down we were meant to be together even though he had moved to the other side of the world. I have to say this about myself: I'm not the best at taking a hint.

As soon as I stumbled out of the office, ticket safely ensconced in my handbag, I worried I had made the most expensive mistake of my life: what if I hated Australia? New Zealand? What if I was wrong about the possible romance? What's more I was going to be celebrating Christmas, New Year and my 30th birthday on my own. How depressing was that going to be?

Could someone like me enjoy backpacking around the world? I always wore smart dresses and stilettoes as my outfit of choice. I loved traipsing around castles, palaces, cathedrals, visiting all manner of historical sites. I suspected that castles and palaces were not the main reason why anyone visited Australia. Admittedly, I knew nothing about Australia apart from what I had garnered from watching, The Sullivans, Neighbours and Crocodile Dundee. In other words: not very much.

My fears proved unfounded even though my supposed love interest had by now a new love interest of his own. Faced with a hint that even I couldn't ignore, I threw myself into travelling and discovered I loved Australia – the breath-taking scenery, the beaches that went on for miles and miles, the national parks the size of a European country, the cave paintings thousands of years older than any painting I had ever seen in Europe. I liked the people; I liked the food; I enjoyed meeting fellow travellers, hooking up with them for a while and then moving on. It was as if there was a parallel society existing in Oz, one for us travellers with our own mini transport system; our own network; our own support system.

What's more I was happy – genuinely happy. I lost weight, got a tan and there must have been something in the mix as I enjoyed being Queen Bee on my travels with various admirers buzzing around me. Everywhere I went there seemed to be always someone to flirt with, although, true to form, that was as far as it generally went. It turns out happiness can be a most attractive quality.

Then off to New Zealand for a far too short a stay and the islands of the Pacific. Staying in Fiji and The Cook Islands I felt as if I had landed in paradise, although neither were places where I would want to stay forever despite the pristine beaches and great weather.

Next stop Tahiti. It too was paradise, if only a far more expensive one. Arriving there one hot night, I descended from the airplane while a group of local musicians played on the tarmac and dancers in bright red traditional outfits danced to the beating of drums. It seemed out of this world. I felt as if I had just walked onto the set of a 1950s movie. So much so, I was half-expecting Stewart Granger or Deborah Kerr to make an appearance

It was also a place where, for once, the British weren't hated. That was reserved for the French. Having lived in France, I might not be as fluent in French as I would have liked, but I spoke it fast and with confidence. Nevertheless, no French person would be under any illusion that it was my mother tongue. A French friend had once confided to me that when I spoke French I sounded like a German Jewish housewife, another that I sounded Belgian. I assumed neither assessment was a compliment. Native Tahitians didn't seem to pick up on what I considered to be a glaringly obvious linguistic fact. I soon learnt in order to get on their good side I had to make it obvious I wasn't French. I got into the habit of interrupting mid-speech whatever I was saying, mumbling out loud in English, how do you say that in French? In the meantime, I would look as if I was concentrating really, really hard, and only then would I carry on speaking French. It worked like a treat.

'You're not French?' would be the immediate response.

'No, British,' I would reply, and the change in how I was treated was instantaneous.

Now I was in the States. It was the final leg of my tour. Home was in sight. I had spent most of that day walking around San Francisco, visiting all the tourist traps, earmarked in my battered copy of the Rough Guide to the USA. Trees were in blossom, and I had enjoyed my wander around the city, soaking up the sights along with the sun. Kitted out in a dark pink summer's dress, a cheap pair of sunglasses, blocking out said sun and giving everything a sepia tint, my white crocheted cardigan that I had brought along with me in true British fashion 'just in case' was proving surplus to requirements.

San Francisco had a more European feel to it than the little I had seen of America so far. I couldn't pinpoint exactly why that was. Maybe it was because using public transport didn't seem to be an alien concept here, as it seemed to be everywhere else in California.

After a long day of sightseeing, I took the train back to the little town where I was staying. I had met an American girl in Tahiti who had committed the rookie error of inviting a total stranger to stay if they should ever be passing. I had taken her up on her offer. It was free accommodation and as my mini world trip was coming to an end, my budget was tight. It was obvious that I had outstayed my welcome, a fact I was studiously ignoring, and one she was far too polite to bring up.

When I had first arrived to stay, Paige had always accompanied me into town and shown me the sights. Today I had been left to my own devices. It was a subtle hint, but a hint nonetheless. I was untroubled by the thought of being left to wander around by myself. I enjoyed my own company. I had travelled around half the world by this point. What could possibly go wrong?

It was early evening when I took the local train back to the non-descript town where Paige lived. I headed to the taxi rank. As was customary in California, taking public transport from the station to Paige's house was out of the question. I had learnt this basic rule more or less the moment I had stepped onto American soil.

My first experience of life in America had been the Greyhound Bus Station in East LA. Looking around me as I arrived at the bus station, I seemed to be the only white face in town; everyone else was either Hispanic or African-American. I didn't fit in. That was obvious from the way I dressed, to the mountains of luggage that surrounded me, to the look of utter bewilderment on my face. I might as well have had a sign on my forehead saying 'mug me I'm a tourist' written in bold.

Of course, I didn't know all this as I stepped inside the Greyhound Bus Station, having managed to haul myself and my luggage into the building. Once inside, I was struck by the fact that the waiting room was fenced off and guarded. In a bus station? That didn't bode well. I noticed too how well-armed the guards were. Firstly, guards? With weapons? At a bus station? Coming from Britain where your average British Bobby has to make do with a truncheon, I was concerned that if the supposed good guys were this heavily armed, what kind of weapons did the bad guys have? In the midst of my pondering and my confusion, a Mexican avocado farmer took pity on me, helped me buy my ticket and saw me safely inside the waiting room.

First stop was San Luis Obispo where I was staying for a few days before I headed further north. It didn't take long for panic to set in as we trundled up the highway and the penny dropped that numerous places where we were stopping at didn't have bus stations as I assumed they would. You were simply dropped off at a stop on the road. By now, it was night and San Luis Obispo was still hours away. What if the guy I was meant to be staying with in SLO wasn't there? After all, I had met him for a mere three days, several weeks previously when I was backpacking in Oz. What if he wasn't there and the stop was just some bus stop in the middle of nowhere? I didn't even have an address for him - just details of a post box where I could send him mail.

Hence my relief was palpable when the coach finally arrived at San Luis Obispo and it pulled into an actual bus station. What's more the SLO guy, as I referred to him in my head for some reason, was there to meet me. He seemed to be the only person there, half-snoozing in a chair. One more generous traveller whose offer of hospitality I was shamelessly taking advantage of.

All things considered, in comparison to my first trip by public transport in the States, the train journey to and from San Francisco had proved a lot less troublesome. I approached the first available taxi and as I did so, the driver smiled and told me in heavily accented English to come and sit in the front. Mistake number one: I know now if a taxi driver asks you to sit in the front with him, NEVER get in the taxi.

Unaware of this golden rule, I assumed he was being friendly. I jumped into the front seat, took out the slip of paper Paige had left for me that morning and gave him the address. I commented on his accent; it was hard to ignore. He told me his name was Ivan and he was originally from Bulgaria. He was a bear of a man, his body almost spilling out of his seat. I was tempted to ask if he'd been an Olympic shot putter in his youth. He had the build of someone who had been immensely strong and fit when he was younger, but had maybe dabbled in too many steroids and his muscles were now turning to fat.

Wisely deciding against making such a bon mot, I babbled on about how I was from London, travelling solo on a round-the-world trip, staying with someone I had just met for a few days on my travels and I was back to San Luis Obispo in the morning. In London, I wouldn't give a complete stranger the time of day.

My modus operandi whenever importuned in my home city was to pretend not to speak English and mutter a few sentences in German at my would-be interlocutor. In my experience, it was a most effective ploy, given that very few fellow Brits speak German as a second language. Once or twice, I had even applied this tactic when accosted on the tube while engrossed in the evening newspaper: apparently unable to speak the language, but sufficiently proficient to do the crossword. All in all, I would never have made a convincing spy. Yet here I was telling a complete stranger what I was up to. But when you're travelling, you have a false sense of security: the belief that when you're on holiday nothing bad can happen to you. The belief that you can be open to people in a way you wouldn't be at home because, what the hell, you're never going to see them again.

Ivan seemed friendly enough, we chatted back and forth, and it wasn't long before he parked up outside a house. For the life of me I couldn't be sure if it was Paige's house or not. There were no lights on in the house but, then again, Paige had said she'd be out for most of the day hence why she couldn't accompany me into town. I had never seen the house from outside late at night, and I had never paid that much attention any time Paige had driven us back home. I looked to see if I could see the house number. Nope: there didn't seem to be one on the house. Maybe it was on the mail box? Nope: a mail box was nowhere to be seen either. I hesitated.

Looking around, it was all so different from a British town. We might be in a residential area, but there was no pavement to step out on, no street lighting, no passers-by. The whole street was shrouded in darkness. If I got out, and it wasn't where Paige lived, I would have no way of finding the right house. There was no way of contacting Paige; there was no one to ask. If I made the wrong decision that was it. I was screwed.

Ivan watched me as I sat in the front seat, my eyes darting around, desperately trying to make out something that looked familiar.

'Are you sure this is it? I can't see the house number?' I asked.

'Give me paper with address.'

I handed over the paper and continued to look around me.

'This address,' he said.

'Are you sure? It doesn't look right somehow '

I grabbed back the piece of paper and read out loud what Paige had written on it.

'Are you sure it's here?'

'Yes. Can you see house?'

I wasn't sure I could. Not in this light. Why was there no damn house number? I was beginning to panic. Before I could think what to do next, Ivan drove off in silence. Where was he going? I looked out the window. No one was about. There weren't even any other cars on the road. We were driving down a dark street in silence to goodness knows where. I forced myself to seem calm. Whatever I do I mustn't show fear I told myself.

I had learnt that trick many moons ago while living in Paris. One night I had gone to watch a triple bill of the Sisi films at a cinema in the République, a district just down the road from me. The Sisi films were a series of films that purported to depict the life of the Empress Elizabeth, Austria's answer to Princess Diana, if from a previous century and with longer hair. I had presumed they would be in the original German with French subtitles. That was my excuse to myself for going to watch them: it was a way of keeping up my German rather than me just wanting to watch some schmaltzy films. Unfortunately, all three films were dubbed into French. I might have lived twice as long in Paris as I had in Vienna but my French wasn't half as good. I had understood very little of what was said, but having paid for my ticket, I was damned if I wasn't going to stay till the bitter end.

It was the early hours of the morning by the time I left the cinema. Rather than take a taxi, I had decided to walk home to my tiny flat off the Boulevard Voltaire. I was far too tight to splash out on a cab despite the lateness of the hour. As I walked along the street, I was joined by a young guy whose first mistake was to ask me if I was English. I knew that like most French people he used the adjective incorrectly to mean British, but being of Scottish stock, I refused to condone such blatant ignorance. 'Non, je ne suis pas anglaise,' I replied. He threw some other nationalities my way – allemande, hollandaise, belge, suisse, italienne. 'Non,' was invariably the reply. Having given up on finding out where I was from, he continued to talk to me: what was I doing? Where was I going? Didn't I know it was dangerous to be walking out this late at night on my own? Did I have a boyfriend? Where was he? I couldn't shake him off. I decided if he continued to walk with me all the way down the road I would not turn off down my street, but instead continue on to Nation and ring the doorbell of a mate who lived on the main boulevard there and ask her for help.

He continued to accompany me for several minutes, and then suddenly turned towards me, his face close to mine and asked me if I was scared. Of course, I was scared. It was late at night: no one else was about and I was by myself with some bloke who I didn't know who was insisting on walking home with me. 'Non,' I replied and gave him a look as if to say it was the stupidest thing I had ever heard in my life, which was quite a feat given that I had fielded questions from British tourists while working as a holiday rep in Majorca in the 1980s. He looked at me for a moment, shrugged his shoulders and walked off. I was relieved, but I couldn't quite believe that it had been that easy to get rid of him. Is that what a man like him feeds on – fear? Is it just no fun otherwise?

Now, sat in the taxi, I was wondering where the hell we were driving to, my anxiety was increasing and my stomach was turning summersaults, but I was determined to seem nonchalant. Yet, I couldn't help taking turns to look out my side of the window, then out through the windscreen and then past Ivan to the little corner of window I could see at his side, desperately hoping I could spot a place or building I might recognise.

'Where are you going?' I asked.

'We drive round and see if you recognise house,' he replied, as if he could read my mind. He switched off the meter. 'No charge.'

What was I going to recognise? It was pitch black outside.

'Take me back to the train station, please,' I suggested.

That seemed to make the most sense to me. I could wait there. It would be safe. I'd be surrounded by people and I should be able to call Paige from there. Meanwhile, my inner panic stations were on full alert. We seemed to be driving further out of town. That couldn't be right. I was desperately trying to think how I could extricate myself from the situation I found myself in.

'The station. Can you take me to the train station, please?'

'What you do there? At station,' he replied and grinned.

'I could wait till my friend gets back home and phone her to come and get me.'

'No phones there,' he replied.

That seemed highly unlikely, but this was America. What did I know? I'd had fun trying to ring SLO man from LA under the mistaken belief that would be regarded as a 'local' call. After all, how big could California be? Very big as I soon found out.

'Well, take me to the police station,' I suggested.

'Police? This America. I cannot take you there. What they do?' he answered back.

He might have a point I thought. American cops weren't like British ones. I knew that much. I thought of an old Dave Allen joke whose conceit was that if you asked a British policeman the time, he would tell you it. You ask an American cop the time, he'd tell you to fuck off.

'Well, let's stop and I'll ask one of the neighbours.'

'This America,' Ivan replied. 'You cannot walk up to door. They shoot you.'

He had a point again. Only a few weeks previously some poor Japanese tourist had been shot dead doing exactly that. I scoured the streets. It was so unlike a British town. Things we took for granted didn't exist here. Not only was there no street lighting, no pavements, no passers-by, but no bus stops, no late-night corner shops or tube stations. No familiar markers you could use as a guide or as a refuge if you needed one.

The panic was setting in now. He had point blank refused to drop me off at any of the places I had suggested; and where the hell was he driving me to anyway? I picked up a map that was wedged between the front seats. I switched the car light on and somehow managed to find the street I was supposed to be staying at. I spotted we were passing a mass of water that lay in the opposite direction of where Paige lived. If I was right, we were heading away from her side of town.

While the dread inside me intensified, conversely, I felt an overbearing need to be nice to him, a need which at the same time infuriated the hell out of me. I didn't want to be nice to him. Ideally, I would have liked to have punched him in the face and jumped out of the car, but he was huge and well-built and could have swatted me like a fly. And jump out to where? Where could I go? I had no idea where I was and no idea how to get to safety. For a second, I toyed with the idea of forcing the car onto oncoming traffic. A crash. He'd have to stop then. Would that work? Minutes later the lights of a solitary oncoming car headed towards us; I realised I didn't have the guts to take such a risk. I felt crushed.

Faced with no other options, my survival instinct kicked in and told me I had to be nice to him. If I was nice to him then maybe he wouldn't harm me. He'd realise how nice I was and leave me alone. I could be charming. I was attractive. I would have to rely on that. At the same time, I couldn't believe this was happening to me. I had done the right thing: I had taken a licensed cab. Surely these guys were vetted. Yet I was being driven goodness knows where by someone who refused to take me to where I wanted to go and refused to let me out of the car.

He eventually turned off the main road and drove down a rutted path which intersected a forest to our right. Stopping in a clearing, he parked the car under a massive tree: he gave a deep sigh as the car shuddered to a halt. This is it: I am going to be raped and murdered: my body will probably never be found. I'll be one more statistic. One more missing woman. Then I spotted the car phone. In my best posh English, I asked him if I could ring Paige to let her know what's happening. After all, I didn't want to worry her. Without waiting for an answer, amidst a profusion of thank yous, I rang Paige's number. The voicemail kicked in and I quickly left a message.

'Hi, it's me. I'm with Ivan the Bulgarian Taxi Driver.'

I made sure that piece of information was on tape. If I was going to be murdered, I wanted them to know who the fucker was who did it. 'I'm in his taxi. We can't find your house for some reason, but he's helping me to find you.'

Ivan must have cottoned on to the possible ramifications of what I had done. After all, it was hardly in code and his English wasn't that basic. It must have sunk in that someone somewhere would know who I was with and when. Seconds later, he reversed the car and we were back off down the path and back on the main road. Within minutes we were outside the house we had first stopped at.

'This it,' he said, pointing at the house.

'Are you sure?'

'Yes.'

By this stage I didn't care if it was the right house or not. I had rather risk getting shot at by a neighbour than stay one more second in the car with him. I jumped out the car and to my horror he squeezed himself out of his side of the car too and stood next to me blocking my escape down the front path.

'You go back to San Luis Obispo tomorrow. Yes? I drive you,' he informed me, with a massive grin on his face as if he was salivating over a juicy steak.

'It's all right. My *boyfriend* has bought me a bus ticket already. I might as well use it.'

I stressed the word boyfriend in the hope he'd back off even if it was a chronic exaggeration of my relationship with SLO man.

'That's OK, no need pay. I take you for free. Much better than bus.'

Was he kidding? He'd more or less kidnapped me, taken me to a forest and now he thought I would want to get back in the car with him.

'That's very kind of you, but I don't think my *boyfriend* would like it.'

At this he sidled up so his body was almost touching mine. I could see from the look on his face he was enjoying the situation: the power. I might be trying my best to seem outwardly calm, but he sensed I was scared. I still had to play nice. I was so close to escaping his clutches. I just needed to get indoors.

'You invite me in?' He pointed at the house.

'No, I'm fucking not!' was the response which formed in my head. However, for once in my life, I made the effort of translating my thoughts into more polite words.

'I'm sorry. It's not my house. I can't invite anyone in without asking Paige first. It would be incredibly rude.'

He sidled up even closer, put out his arm and began to feel up my breasts. I wanted to scream and tell him to fuck off, punch him in the face, do something, but the only weapon I had was playing fucking nice. After all, if I tried anything, he could knock me sideways with the flick of his wrist. And he knew it. What's more, he knew that *I* knew it. All I could think about was that I had to get out of here at any cost. If this was the price that I had to pay then I had to pay it and be thankful that I had got off so lightly.

'Thanks for all your help, *Ivan*,' I said as loud as I could, ignoring what he had just done to me. 'Thanks for being such a helpful *taxi driver*,' I shouted. 'Bye.'

I turned and steeled myself to walk calmly to the door: walk normally I kept telling myself over and over again. He mustn't see how scared I am. If I run, I was sure of it: he'll follow me inside. If I walk normally, I've more of a chance. I fumbled at the door with the key, expecting any minute to hear his footsteps coming down the path. If I did, I decided I would start screaming. I would scream the whole neighbourhood down for as long as I could. Finally, the key was in the lock, the door opened and I was inside the house. I slammed the door shut, leaning against it, unable to believe my luck. I was safe.

Forty minutes later, Paige and her sister Sydney arrived home. I recounted events as if it had all happened to someone else. It was as if I had already disassociated myself from the 'me' who had experienced it.

'Do you want to call the cops?' Sydney asked.

'No,' I replied.

That came as a shock. I had always considered myself to be the type of woman who would call the police if something like this ever happened to her: moreover, that you had a duty to report something like this. At school, at work, I had always been the bolshie one: the one to stand up and be counted. The unofficial trade union rep. At sweet sixteen I was working as a cashier when management decided one Christmas to take away all the chairs in order for us to work faster. I refused. The only one. The manager came up to me at the till.

'The chair has to go,' she informed me.

'No, it doesn't. Legally, I'm entitled to one.'

I flicked open the staff handbook which I had made sure was to hand and pointed to the relevant paragraph.

The manager took one look at it, saw the determination sketched in my face, sighed and walked off. I kept my chair.

Yet here I was and the last thing I wanted to do was talk to the police about it: to go through it all again. I wanted it behind me. I didn't even want to think about it. As it was, I was leaving town tomorrow to spend a week with a man whose company I enjoyed. I didn't want to hang around here making statements to the police.

What's more I was leaving the States in a couple of weeks' time. What good would it do anyway? It would be my word against his. And what had he done really? He'd driven me around in his taxi, refused to let me out, driven me to a forest, drove me back to where I needed to go and felt up my tits. He would argue that he had been trying to help me find where I was staying; he'd touched me by accident and I was some neurotic woman who'd watched one too many crime shows.

Even if it went to court, I was hardly going to be popping back to the States for some trial any time soon; presumably to be asked how short the dress was that I had been wearing that night; if I had been drinking; what underwear I had on and how many men I had slept with. Despite the fact that my dress had reached my knees, I don't drink, my knickers were spectacularly uninteresting ones from BHS and I could count the men I had slept with on one hand, I was pretty certain that somehow it would still end up having been all my fault.

'Are you sure you don't want to report it?' Sydney asked.

'Yes. Most definitely,' I replied.

'What I don't understand,' Paige said, 'is how you didn't recognise the house.'

'I've never seen it in the dark and I couldn't see the house number anywhere,' I explained. It felt somehow as if Paige was laying part of the blame for what had happened, on me.

'But it's on the mailbox,' Paige said.

'What mailbox? I couldn't see any mailbox outside the house,' I replied. What did she think I did? Spotted the number and decided to go on a mini road trip with a Bulgarian sociopath for the hell of it.

'Oh, I see. The mailbox isn't outside our house. It's on the opposite side of the street with a few of the others,' Paige explained.

What the fuck? Who the hell has their mail box on the opposite side of the fucking street?

The next morning, I briefly mentioned what happened to me while I was on the phone to SLO man before I set off back to his place. Maybe I downplayed it, I don't know, but we never mentioned it. I was so relieved to see him, I didn't care. Here was a man the total opposite of the taxi driver. It was the tonic I needed: to be in male company that was kind, considerate and caring.

After that day I did what most women do when something bad has happened to them. I never told a soul. I locked it away with all the other bad things that had happened to me. My own personal treasure trove of times when someone, somewhere, has felt entitled to try and own me, possess me, force themselves on me, touch me, scare me or humiliate me. I hid it away so deep that you kid yourself you've forgotten about it and then something happens: you're out one night and someone follows you out of the tube; you're walking home late one evening and a car comes to a halt beside you, the engine still running, as the driver rolls down the window and offers to give you a lift, when you refuse, he flies into a rage, calling you names and calling you out; you're in a bar and a guy blocks your path and harangues you for not wanting to talk to him or letting him buy you a drink, as if it's your personal fault that he's single. That's when the contents from your own personal treasure trove start to rise and circulate throughout your body, and the fear begins to grab you by the throat, and you try and stay calm; you might even feel the need to play nice – despite everything – despite every sinew in your body crying out for you to fight, to hit out whatever the odds, but sometimes you don't because you're scared and they are stronger than you, and you want to survive. And what's the worst thing about it? You know for you and for every other woman around the world this is just an ordinary day.

A Day at the Beach

How things had changed since she was a kid. For starters, they were holidaying abroad. In her youth, their family holidays seemed to alternate between Cornwall and Scotland. They were apparently the only two options in the 1970s. Cornwall and Scotland. That was as exotic as it got, staying in caravans or youth hostels, although admittedly they had once gone upmarket and stayed in a chalet. For Joyce and her brother Alan that had seemed the height of luxury.

Some things had apparently not changed however. Just as her dad had done for her and Alan, Joyce watched as her partner built yet another car in the sand for the kids. The kids, in all their excitement, were hindering more than they were helping, while Joyce 'supervised' proceedings and warded off an intrusive seagull from the remnants of her ice cream, part of which was already leaving a white sticky trail down her hand. Just your average day at the beach.

That's what they had called it back then too: A Day at the Beach. Fifty odd years ago, that phrase had another meaning for Joyce and her little gang. At first, it had been an innocuous sounding phrase, but thanks to fate, bad luck and her own culpability, it now reminded her of the moment when she had first realised that life wasn't fair. Bad things can happen to good people. This harmless sounding expression encapsulated a chain of events whose repercussions had trickled down through her childhood, and had blighted her adulthood.

The beach in question back then had been some builders' sand left at the bottom of their road in a not too salubrious part of North London, where, thanks to a dip in the road, a pool of rainwater had collected next to it. In their minds, children of the 1970s brought up with lots of imagination, very little telly and no internet or mobile phones, this was the perfect replica of the seaside. No day spent outside playing in the streets would be complete without a visit to the beach. It being summer, every day was spent playing outside, weather permitting.

How childhoods had changed in those intervening years. Joyce wouldn't countenance for a moment the kids playing out front. For starters, who would they play with? She was only on nodding acquaintance with some of the neighbours at best, let alone going in and out of each other's houses as her parents had done when she was a child. In the 1970s, children played in the streets from morning to night, only stopping for lunch - usually a jam sandwich or as her family insisted on calling it a 'jelly piece', and then back to the serious work of playing. Sweets made to look like cigarettes so you could pretend to smoke them. A slap with a wooden spoon if your parents felt you deserved it. At eight, Joyce was the oldest and therefore had unilaterally decided to be the ringleader of their little gang, a year younger was their neighbour's son, Patrick, then her own brother, Alan, and lastly, Patrick's brother, Sean, the youngest, aged 4.

Parenting had been very different back then too. Joyce's parents had been Scottish Presbyterians who had come down to London in the early 1960s in search of a better life. In those days, parents drank, parents smoked and most believed in leaving the children to their own devices once they were old enough to play outside.

Most of the neighbours were Irish Catholics from the South of Ireland who had come to London for the exact same reason as Joyce's parents had. It might have been the time of the Troubles in Northern Ireland but this was London and nobody cared about anyone's religious affiliations. After all, Joyce's parents might be Scottish Presbyterians, Patrick's Irish Catholics but they had one thing in common: they both had to put up with being treated like second-class citizens thanks to being Celts. The fact that they were fellow Celts overrode any other considerations.

The Maguires were far better off than the Balfours. Even as a child, Joyce had been aware of that. The Maguire house was one of the first on their street to have pebbledash, although it presumably helped that the Maguires ran their own building company. The Maguires also had that most prized of possessions: a colour television set. As a special treat, the Balfour children were allowed to go to the Maguires to watch The High Chaparral in colour every Friday evening.

Joyce loved The High Chaparral. It featured her second ever TV crush, Henry Darrow as Manolito. Joyce supposed she was meant to fancy

Billy Blue Cannon but Manolito was the one for her although she was torn from having to split both her loyalties and her affection with her first ever cowboy crush, Doug McClure alias Trampas in The Virginian. His poster, cut out from a magazine, still took pride of place on the wall above her bed.

In the 1970s, families from different cultural backgrounds had markedly different houses. Once the Maguires eventually left the street, Joyce befriended her next-door neighbour's youngest daughter, Claudette. Her family was Bajan and this is when Joyce first encountered locked front rooms, filled with ornaments and brightly coloured, crotched swan doilies on any surface where they could be placed and the pièce de résistance, the sofa covered in a sheet of plastic.

As for Irish houses, it seemed to Joyce that Irish parents said 'feck' a lot. This apparently meant they were not swearing although it sounded a lot like swearing to Joyce. Joyce had once said feck, and she had been suitably reprimanded with the back of a wooden spoon on her bare leg by her mother. Joyce found this a tad unfair: not only did Mrs Maguire say 'feck' all the time but her mother wasn't averse to the odd swear word herself. It was also in the Maguire house that Joyce came face to face for the first time with a Catholic priest, sat in an armchair, drinking whisky AND smoking. Joyce couldn't imagine for one second the Minister at St Columba's, the sparse Scottish Presbyterian Church in Central London that her family occasionally attended, ever doing anything like that. It was also the first time Joyce had ever encountered a painting of Jesus Christ, bearing his heart with barbed wire around it. At first glance, Joyce found the picture scary and unsettling but the lure of watching The High Chaparral in colour soon overrode any qualms on that score.

Her last day at the impromptu beach on their street had started like any other day. She and her brother had breakfast; they had squabbled for a bit then the doorbell rang. Patrick and Sean were standing on the front steps and, without further ado, Joyce and Alan bounded outside. It didn't take long for Patrick and Alan to be stuck into their favourite game of playing toy soldiers in the Balfour's front garden while Joyce and Sean decided to go for a walk to the beach.

Before they set off, Joyce decided to bring along her favourite doll. Joyce remembered the doll as being huge, almost as tall as Sean. She had been given to Joyce as a present 'from her brother' the day he had been born. Joyce's parents had hoped that the doll's arrival would stop Joyce from becoming jealous of the new addition to the family. As it turned out Joyce was never jealous of the new arrival. If anything, Alan had been jealous of her but the doll had been a big success. Joyce and Sean each took a hand of the doll as they played parents taking their child to the beach. They walked down the street, crossed the road, sat down on the kerb and kicked their feet in the sand. Dolly was placed between them.

Joyce had hoped the others would be tempted to come too but they hadn't been. Sean was only four and she soon got bored. 'I'm going to walk Dolly up the street,' she said. At that age, walking up the street seemed a massive adventure. 'Are you coming?'

'No,' Sean said. 'I want to stay at the beach.'

'OK,' Joyce said. 'Let's go,' she said turning to Dolly.

Joyce walked up the road as far as she was allowed to go and then crossed over keeping a wary eye on the older kids at number 83 who, for some reason, nobody knew precisely why, Joyce and co weren't allowed to play with. Joyce had just passed them when suddenly there was a loud bang, emanating from down the road. Seconds later the kids at number 83 were running full pelt down the road. Joyce wasn't sure what was happening but she sensed something was and dragging Dolly behind her, she followed as fast as she could.

Outside the Maguire's there was total pandemonium. Her mother and father were standing outside the Maguires' house as was Patrick and Alan. Mrs Maguire was in hysterics as she watched Mr Maguire walk towards them, in his arms, Sean, unconscious with blood streaming all over him, his head hanging at an unnatural angle to the rest of his body. A man Joyce had never seen before, was standing beside a car, parked in the middle of the road with the driver's door wide open. The man was wailing something but Joyce was unable to make out what it was.

As Mr Maguire approached, Joyce's dad turned sharply and told all the children they had to go inside number 29 now. Mum was usually the scary one but this time it was clear her father meant business. His gruff, dour manner helped in no small measure to get the message home.

Once inside the house Mrs Balfour explained that Sean had been hurt and needed to go to hospital. 'Is he hurt bad?' Patrick asked, trying to hold back the tears. Mr and Mrs Balfour didn't answer directly but poured the kids some squash, bribed them with a couple of Penguin biscuits and a Wagon Wheel each and told them to go upstairs and play. Joyce decided she had to do something to save the day. After all, she was the eldest. There was only one thing to do: she would pray to God. She locked herself in the loo, closed her eyes, put her hands together and assured God that if he made sure that Sean wasn't too badly hurt, she would never say shut up again. In order to seal the deal, she promised never to ask for a Disney magazine ever again either, and she would give those she already had to Sean. They were her most prized possessions. A deal like that would be impossible for God to refuse, she reckoned, and suitably reassured that Sean would be OK, she joined Alan and Patrick in re-enacting the last episode of The High Chaparral that they had watched, using the big toy box their dad had made for their communal bedroom as the ranch.

Hours passed. Dinner was served. As a special treat, Findus Crispy Pancakes were served up. As a further special treat, ice cream was offered for dessert. This was unheard of. Ice cream was only ever a Sunday treat. It might have been just a few hours since Sean had had to go away but for the children it seemed like a lifetime. They were torn between wondering why Sean was talking so long to get better and enjoying the unusual fuss the Balfour parents were making over them. As it got later and later, there was still no sign of Mr Maguire and Sean. Even more confusing for the Balfour children was that their parents didn't seem to mind them staying up so late for once. What Mr and Mrs Balfour did seem to be uncomfortable about was whenever Patrick would ask about his dad coming to pick him up. The later it got, the more often the question was asked. Finally, there was a knock on the door. Joyce's dad got up and told the children to stay where they were. He opened the front door, and mere seconds later, heedless of what he had just told them, all the children were gathered around him, desperate to see Sean. Standing on the threshold, blocking out the last rays of a summer's evening sun, stood Mr Maguire but no Sean.

'Come along, Patrick,' he said. 'We need to go home.'

'Is Sean at home?' Joyce enquired, pushing forward past her father. 'I have some magazines for him. If you wait, Mr Maguire, I'll get them now. Could you give them to him, please?'

Without waiting for a reply, Joyce turned on her heels and sped up the stairs. Mr Maguire stood stock-still and stared at Mr and Mrs Balfour. No words were needed. Everything that needed to be said was written on Mr Maguire's face.

'Come along, Patrick. There's a good boy,' Mr Maguire said. Mrs Balfour stifled a cry while Mr Balfour, unable to express his emotions at the best of times, stood stony faced. Having by now arrived back down the stairs, a pile of magazines encased in her arms, Joyce watched as Mr Maguire took Patrick up in his arms and walked towards the front gate. Having evidently said something to Patrick as they walked along, Patrick started sobbing and rested his head on his dad's shoulder as his dad walked him down the road.

Joyce ran down the front steps and followed them down the road despite her father's attempt to catch hold of her as she passed him. Joyce was determined to keep her end of the bargain. She knew how important it was that she did.

'Mr Maguire, don't forget the magazines for Sean. Mr Maguire,' Joyce called down the street.

Mr Maguire kept on walking.

'Come on in, Joyce,' her father urged as he walked towards her.

'But you don't understand,' Joyce tried to explain. She was beginning to panic. 'I've got to give these magazines to Sean.'

'Sean won't be needing those magazines, Joyce.' Her father was fumbling with his words. How do you explain what he had to explain to a child?

'But you don't understand, daddy. I need to give them to him. It's really, really important.'

Her father bent down to speak to her.

'Sean's not at home.'

'Where is he then? Is he still at the hospital?'

Joyce tried to think back as to what her exact agreement with God had been.

'No, Joyce.' Her father's voice, tremulous for once, interrupted her thoughts. 'I'm afraid Sean has had to go to heaven.'

'Why?' was all that Joyce could think to say.

What happened next was a blur. The one thing Joyce could remember was her utter disbelief that God hadn't accepted her deal. It had been a fair enough swap. Why hadn't he agreed? Hadn't she offered enough? What else could she have done?

A week later, they saw Sean in his coffin. Joyce was struck by the fact that it didn't look anything like him. His hair was all wrong and it looked as if he had make up on. The Balfour family went to the funeral where they grappled with their grief and the insistence of a Catholic Church service of never being able to make up its mind as whether you should sit, stand or kneel.

Life went on but it was never the same. Unable to live in the street where their child had been killed, the Maguires soon moved and they lost touch with the Balfours. For years, Joyce wondered what would have happened if she had stayed and played with Sean or insisted he went up the road with her. Did the Maguires suspect she was to blame? Is that why they had moved? Is that why they had lost touch with the family? Was it her fault? How can one apparently insignificant decision have such tragic consequences?

She looked at the kids playing in the sand and remembered the terror she felt when she realised that she was going to be a parent for the first time. So many things could go wrong. One simple mistake and the consequences were unimaginable. It had made her think twice about getting together with Pete as soon as he mentioned he was a single dad with two young kids. Pete initially thought it was this extra baggage which he had that was the problem. It wasn't the children per se. Joyce and the kids had hit it off from the start. As Joyce knew only too well, kids tended to like Joyce. All her friends' kids had a soft spot for her. She always ended up being the one adult in the room playing with them. No, that wasn't the problem. The problem was the responsibility that came with being a parent. That was the problem. The fear of making a wrong decision. What might happen if she screwed up again. She didn't want a second child on her conscience.

'Did you ever want kids of your own?' Pete had once asked her.

'No,' she said.

He looked at her surprised.

'It's just I thought most women do,' he explained.

Joyce said nothing. She smiled and shook her head. Her silent attempt to disabuse him of that particular belief. Meanwhile, she thought to herself, 'That was another bargain I made with God.'

Read on for the three stories first published under the following collection:

The

Void

MAUREEN YOUNGER

DEDICATION

Für die Burschen

ACKNOWLEDGMENTS

To Jen Brister, Jayne Phenton and VG Lee for their unstinting assistance, support and patience.

VIENNA

'No man ever steps in the same river twice, for it's not the same river and he's not the same man.' Heraclitus

****

There is always a strange feeling when you go back to a city that was once your home. You know the city as it was, but not as it is. You think of your friends there as they once were and not as they have become and, more importantly, you think of yourself as you wished you had remained. In her case, that was young, carefree and with her life still ahead of her, unaware of all the possibilities and opportunities she would blithely disregard. Ignorant of all the time she would waste. All the time she was still wasting.

It was as if she'd left a life there she could have lived and now she was back; the city and the people had moved on, and everything was just ever so slightly out of sync.

These thoughts scurried through her mind as she looked around Vienna's West Station and felt something was amiss and not just the fact that he hadn't turned up to meet her as promised. After thirty years he could have been on time or at least sent a text to say where he was.

Nevertheless, she continued to look around the station hoping against hope that he was there. West Station. She couldn't remember exactly how it looked when she'd first come to Vienna in 1984, but it certainly had never looked like this nor had it been so spacious. Now it merely seemed to be another excuse for a shopping centre.

As if to reassure herself that some things never change, she ignored the numerous modern eateries on offer and headed across the road, rolling her suitcase behind her, across one side of the ring road, appropriately called the Gürtel, the German for belt, over the jumble of tram tracks, over the other side of the Gürtel, to a coffee house in the traditional Viennese style; just how she liked it. She plopped herself down and as soon as the waitress scuttled over, she asked for a melange, her coffee of choice. Minutes later the waitress was back, the melange on a silver tray accompanied by the obligatory glass of water; Austrian style.

She sent off a text telling him where she was and got out her book, an all-time favourite, pacing herself with her coffee as she pretended to read. It was hard to concentrate. She might be looking at the words, but she was thinking of him. Trust him to be late. Maybe some things don't change after all. His unreliability; her stupidity.

She poked around in her handbag, dumping several bits and pieces of its contents next to her coffee on the table, when she finally found what she was looking for: her mirror. She then stuffed the miscellaneous items back into her bag, and snapped the mirror open and looked at her face. Yes, some things do change. She was losing her looks; she had gained weight. That was evident as she stroked the layer of fat under her chin. She raised the mirror higher for a more flattering look: well, at least her cheekbones were still hanging in there. As for her hair, it still refused to adhere to any recognisable hairstyle and up close the brown tint was probably a bit too dark to go with the face. She let out a loud sigh and placed the mirror back in the bag.

Perhaps she should contact another friend in the city, surprise them with her arrival; hint about whether she could stay with them. She had said nothing about her visit to anyone else, feeling embarrassed by the whole affair. Affair - that was an odd choice of words. Their so-called affair thirty years ago had been such an unmitigated disaster, it seemed inaccurate to call it one. So why was she here now?

She looked at her phone. Still no bloody text. She rang, but the phone went straight to voicemail. She had a choice. She could sit here, waiting for him to get in touch and pretend to read her book, or do something. Her natural inclination was to check out some of her old haunts.

In the old days whenever she'd felt at a loss, she would walk from the Josefstadt, where she shared a flat opposite his, to Schönbrunn Palace and walk up the hill to the Gloriette. It was a hell of a walk, but it gave her some kind of aim whenever she was feeling particularly aimless. And she always felt aimless whenever her non-relationship with him had hit an impasse, which was often. Being mid-winter, it was freezing, her nose would go bright red in the cold and it was tiring walking through all that snow and sludge. Somehow the physical exertion helped alleviate the emotional turmoil going on inside her. She'd get to the top of the hill, crowned by The Gloriette, panting as if she were in dire need of oxygen, and survey the formal gardens, covered in snow, leading to the yellow palace below, Austria's answer to Versailles. The very fact she had managed to reach the heady climes of the Gloriette felt like some kind of achievement against the failure of her non-existent love life.

Thirty years on, she decided she'd forget the walking there part and take the tram, at least that way she'd still get to see something of the city. She paid for her melange and trundled back over the Gürtel and tramlines. Having stored her suitcase in one of the lockers at the station, she splashed out on a day ticket and headed for the 58 tram stop. Only to find that like the J-Wagen before it, it had been replaced and she needed the 65. Yet another reminder that she was now out of sync with a city she had once considered home. Minutes later a tram arrived and she jumped on board, looking intently out the windows as the tram sped along.

Once at Schönbrunn, she walked through the gardens and headed straight for the Gloriette. Panting her way to the top again, as in days of yore, having to stop once or twice to get her breath back, she finally stood underneath it, looking down at the summer palace of the Hapsburgs. It was a spectacular memorial to an Empire that no longer existed; a country that had once stretched from the Netherlands to Northern Italy and as far east as parts of present-day Ukraine, and which had been truncated to its German-speaking rump after the First World War. The Empire might be long gone, but Vienna's cornucopia of over-the-top buildings were a visible reminder of the city's imperial past: they were just a bit too big, just a bit too impressive for a country of its size and importance. Like her, they were out of sync with reality. Maybe she was more at home here than she realised.

She stared at the Palace and wondered how much she had changed since she used to come here as a student. She'd come to Vienna originally to study German and Russian. She had duly enrolled as a foreign student at Vienna's grand university, once she had managed to work her way through the maze of Austrian bureaucracy.

This early brush with Austrian officialdom had made her appreciate why Kafka had written the stories he had. As a foreign student you had to register separately from everyone else at the university. She would queue up, hand in her papers, only to be told by a bored admin assistant, 'Ihnen fehlt was'. Evidently, she was missing something, but the admin assistant would never tell her, as a matter of principle, what the thing was that was missing. She'd finally track down what she suspected was the problem, correct it, and with renewed hope she would return to the university and queue back up again, only to be told 'Ihnen fehlt was'.

She soon learnt it was seemingly a deeply-held principle of the country's officialdom that Austrian bureaucrats never told you all the things that were missing in one fell swoop, but rather preferred a more drip-feed approach. That way things took longer, you wasted more time and they had more opportunity to tell you your papers were incorrect. Things improved appreciably once a kind-hearted Austrian took pity on her and explained what a Trafik and Bundesstempelmarken were, both words that had never featured in any of the German she'd learnt over the years. A Trafik, it turned out, was the Austrian for tobacconists. These small shops were dotted all over Vienna and had a handy side line selling tickets and travel cards as well as stamps, which is where the phenomenon of Bundesstempelmarken came in. In the mid-1980s at least, it seemed as if Austrian officialdom was unable to process any paperwork unless a Bundesstempelmarke or two was attached to it.

Finally, she was enrolled and after all that bureaucratic kerfuffle she attended the odd lecture and wisely decided she would learn more German by socialising with Austrians. This proved to be true, although it did little to improve her Russian. It was then she got to know him, in the Café Hummel in the Josefstadt, where in hindsight she realised she'd spent some of the happiest evenings of her youth.

1984: it all seemed a hell of a long time ago and yet it seemed like yesterday. What did she have to show for all those intervening years? Not much. More to the point, why in heaven's name was she still so attached to a city she'd lived in for a mere six months over thirty years ago? Why had she turned up here to meet someone she'd never really been in a proper relationship with, although at the time she had convinced herself that this was 'it' – the grand romance?

There is something addictive about unrequited love. It can last for years, every rejection feeding your habit, placing you firmly in the crosshair between low self-esteem and self-delusion. Convinced that if only the object of your affection would realise how right *you* were for *them,* then how happy *they* would be. If only they knew how much you loved them, surely, they would fall at your feet. Often, it's the fact that *you* don't know *them* which helps fuel the addiction. Unrequited love works best when the beloved doesn't live anywhere near you, preferably abroad and above all else is emotionally unavailable, at least to you.

Obviously, you refuse to accept they are emotionally unavailable through self-deception, misunderstanding and sheer persistence. It's easy. Whenever they say something you don't want to hear, you tell yourself they mean the opposite. He doesn't want a girlfriend? As far as you're concerned, what he's really saying is that he doesn't want a girlfriend *apart* from you. The truth? He wouldn't mind a girlfriend, just *not* you!

Why do this to ourselves? Is it self-hate? Is it fear? Have we set ourselves impossible ideals to such an extent that a non-relationship suits our needs much better than an actual relationship, subject to all its faults and failures?

'Oh, Christ,' she thought. This was too much internalising. She would concentrate on something far more palpable. Feeling hungry, she made her way to a restaurant she knew.

It wasn't that close. A good 20-minute walk at least, but she needed to keep busy. It was packed as usual, but there was still one empty table outside at the back so she made her way over, rushing slightly in case some new diner entered and beat her to it. She glanced at the menu, but already knew what she was going to order. The same thing she always ordered: goulash and bread dumplings.

A few minutes after ordering her meal, and once more pretending to be engrossed in her book, she heard a male voice from above summon her attention. For a fleeting moment she thought it might be him, but it couldn't be. He didn't know she was here. She looked up to see a young man, flashing a bright set of white teeth as he smiled down at her.

'May I?' he asked in German as he pointed to the bench opposite hers, and then looked round at the busy tavern as if to say this was the only room in the inn.

'Ja, sicher,' she replied and smiled back. He was a good-looking bloke, tall, fine featured, olive skin with a mop of curly black hair she quickly noted. She closed her book, having decided she would engage him in conversation. Despite all recent proof to the contrary, in her head she sometimes still saw herself as the foxy young thing she'd been in her twenties, and unable to help herself, she began to flirt.

Fortunately, the young man, Agustín, mistook her flirting for simple friendliness; the kind of immediate friendship that two foreigners strike up when meeting in a foreign land.

She soon learnt he was from Mexico, 24 years old, happily engaged to an Austrian which was how he had ended up working in Lambach in Upper Austria where the hardest part of his job was trying to understand the local dialect. She commiserated with him, and they talked about Austria, Vienna, what an idiot the American president was and how, if he liked great countryside, Agustín should visit Scotland.

It was only when they were sipping their coffees, she another melange, he an espresso, it hit her that the conversation they were having was like the conversations she used to have when she was a student in Vienna. Neither had looked at their phone, checked their social media or taken a call. They had spent an hour and a half conversing and enjoying each other's company.

It also hit her she hadn't once thought of him, he that must not be named, he who had been supposed to meet her almost three hours ago. She hadn't even checked if he'd been in touch. At the thought, she immediately looked at her phone. He hadn't.

As for Agustín, she was aware by now that flirt all she might, he was far too young and she far too old to be regarded as a sexual object by him. This realisation didn't bother her. She recalled how she had been hit on enough times when she was younger by much older men to appreciate it wasn't rejection per se it was just life. And, anyway, she was simply enjoying his company, he was making her laugh and she needed that.

He looked at his watch. 'I need to go into town,' he replied in his American-accented English. They had soon abandoned speaking German once Maureen mentioned she was British.

'Oh of course,' she replied, not quite able to hide the disappointment in her voice.

'I have to meet some friends,' he explained. He hesitated for a moment and catching the waiter's eye, signalled for the bill. Then, turning back towards her, he asked, 'Would you like to come? Or maybe you already have plans?'

'No plans,' she immediately replied and switched off her phone, without even checking the screen, and stuffed it into her handbag.

A few minutes later, having paid, following a rather lengthy discussion of how much tip one should leave (she took a more European view, he more of an American one) they got up to go.

'Your book," Agustín pointed to a well-thumbed copy of Stefan Zweig's A Letter from an Unknown Woman, lying on the table by the empty coffee cup.

She shook her head and scrunched up her nose. 'It's fine. Leave it for someone else.'

'You finished it?' Agustín asked.

'In a way,' she smiled, 'I suppose I have'.

THE NIGHTIE

She hadn't bought a new outfit in years. Walking into her bedroom, this was hard to believe. Two wardrobes in the tiny room were crammed with clothes. Under her bed lay several suitcases, stuffed with even more garments; each one charting her adulthood and the corresponding increase in dress size. A decade ago, she had stopped buying clothes all together, refusing to admit she now needed a size 20. Instead, one by one, the number of clothes she could wear from among her humongous wardrobe had dwindled down to the half dozen or so dresses she could still squeeze into. Thank God for polyester! She told herself that if she didn't buy any clothes, she wouldn't have to admit that she had crossed the Rubicon: size 20 was just one size too far. She had compensated by buying accessories – any size fits after all. Well, apart from bangles.

At times she found it hard to believe that in her youth she had been a size 10 and had possessed a slim figure which she had never appreciated at the time. But from her mid-30s the pounds had accrued gradually and inexorably; month in month out. It was always the same. Every time she reached a weight milestone, she would do a double take. By her mid-30s, she weighed 12 stone and told herself she must lose weight. She didn't. The weight continued to creep up. As she neared her 40th birthday, she tipped the scales at 13 stone. Once more, she said to herself, enough was enough, but it turned out it wasn't, and on the eve of her 50th birthday, she had reached the giddy heights of 16 stone. That really was enough. She envisaged herself being 'featured' on one of those reality TV programmes, something along the lines of '28 Stone Woman Crushed to Death by Her Accessories'. It was time to do the unthinkable and eat healthily!

Until this point, she had remained in denial, aided and abetted by her female friends who were always very supportive when it came to her weight. As a rule, female friends are always supportive - at least to your face. Behind your back the general consensus may be somewhat different. Outwardly, at least, her friends were reassuring and adamant that she didn't look her weight. After all, she was very tall. In reality she wasn't that tall. For someone of her weight, she figured she would probably need to be 9 foot 8 and she was pretty certain, if memory served her right, that at best she was 5 foot 7.

As a child of the 70s - well technically the 60s and the 70s (but she was in denial about her age too) - she had grown up with all the unhealthy eating peccadillos innate to that era. It was an age which embraced the avid consumption of such healthy delights as crispy pancakes, garlic bread and sweets disguised as cigarettes. Then there were the special nights out at a Wimpy. These would invariably include chicken nuggets, chips and, to top the night off in style, a Knickerbocker Glory.

Added to that, despite living in North London, she had grown up in an inveterate Scottish working-class family. This meant that no meal was complete without a considerable amount of high-saturated fat, and where preferably at least one item on the plate – if not all - had been fried. As a child, her biggest culinary treat was when her dad cooked potato fritters for supper.

In those days, among her family at least, the main aim of cooking seemed to be to eliminate any nutritional value the food might possibly contain. True, dessert often consisted of fruit, but always out of a tin, either mandarin segments, pear pieces or if mum was in a particularly exotic mood, fruit cocktail; any nutritional value which might have survived the canning process was then counterbalanced either with ice cream, custard or evaporated milk.

For the last 10 days, however, she had been good and eaten salads, gone out walking and denied herself her usual four cups of coffee a day. As a result, she had lost a whopping five lbs. She conceded it didn't make her Kate Moss, but she was now down to 15 stone 9 and was already imagining the possibility of having the figure she used to have when she was in her early 30s and still a desirable, young woman.

To celebrate surviving 10 days of not eating chocolate, drinking caffeine and late-night eating, she decided to treat herself to a new nightie. Her current set of pyjamas had definitely seen better days.

The back of the trousers sported a cluster of holes of varying sizes and shapes. By anybody's reckoning not the sexiest of looks. She had been single since the heady days of being a size 14 but she now resolved to go back to her former sexy self and to invest in some decent and enticing nightwear.

This proved a more difficult shop than she had imagined. She quickly realised certain shops weren't for her. Much to her annoyance one shop didn't even size the clothes, but just labelled them small, medium and large. She made her way to the counter and asked the shop assistant what size was a large. '12,' the woman replied. 'What?' she asked incredulously. 'A large is a size 12,' the assistant confirmed. 'Not in Britain,' she assured her. 'Have you been down the High Street recently? I think you'll find that to the average Brit a size 12 is wishful thinking.' The shop assistant stared at her blankly.

It was apparent that when it came to buying a nightdress her only options seemed to be between dressing like her grandmother or dressing like a slut. She planned on putting off the former for as long as possible. As for the slut option, she might be down to 15 stone 9, but she knew that still didn't mean she'd look good in a see-through, nylon, baby doll nightie with accompanying frilly, see-through G-string knickers. And then there was the comfort aspect. 'Who the hell would want to wear a pair of G-string knickers to bed?' she thought to herself 'Who the hell would want to wear a pair of G-string knickers full stop?' She'd never understood the attraction. She tried them a couple of times and found them literally bum-numbingly excruciating. So what if people saw your panty line? It just proved you were wearing knickers. Surely that was a good thing, wasn't it?

Then in what seemed like the zillionth shop of the afternoon, and on the verge of giving up, there it was, hanging in front of her, as she wandered into the lingerie department. A lovely black nightie, fringed with cream lace and even better, hidden breast support. She wasn't exactly sure what that was, but it sounded good. What more could you want? 'Hopefully my size!' she said to herself. She couldn't believe her luck. Her size was there. She grabbed the nightie as well as one in the next size down – just in case. 'Well, you never know,' she thought to herself, 'I have lost 5 lbs after all.'

Her luck definitely was in. There was no queue outside the dressing room. There was, however, a gaggle of shop assistants gathered at the entrance, clearly resenting the arrival of a customer interrupting their private and rather lively conversation. Begrudgingly a young Asian girl wearing a headscarf and ensconced in copious amounts of make-up sauntered over.

'Sorry, I didn't see you there,' the shop assistant said as she took the nighties from her, and after counting the two items, handed them back to her along with an electronic tag. 'Dressing room three,' the shop assistant announced and sauntered back to her colleagues. Having taken the proffered tag from the shop assistant, she stared at the two rows of empty dressing rooms, banked against the walls, puzzled as to why the shop assistant was so adamant that she should use that particular dressing room. Nonetheless she went into the allocated dressing room, closed the curtain behind her and started to undress. Staring at herself in the full-length mirror, she had to admit it wasn't a great look, standing there in mismatched knickers and bra, her stomach spilling over in waves around her midriff. She slipped on the nightie in the larger size and immediately felt better about herself. The nightie's A-line shape skimmed her stomach and flattered her silhouette. The hidden breast support pulled her breasts together and gave them shape. Then she tried the smaller size.

Admittedly, deep down she had suspected that although she might technically be able to fit into the smaller size, it probably wouldn't be as flattering. And she had suspected correctly. This one didn't skim her body like the previous one. Her various stomachs rippled through the material. She quickly undressed again, put the larger size back on and confirmed what she already knew. 'Maybe next time,' she thought to herself, glancing at the discarded smaller version lying on the floor by her feet. She took the larger nightie off again and hung it carefully back on to the hanger. She checked the price. £19.50! Her luck really was holding out. The nightie was even reasonably priced.

Not believing her good fortune, she rushed to the cash desk. Once there, she saw with horror that her luck had now taken a turn for the worse. There were three people queuing up ahead of her wanting to return various items. Under normal circumstances she would swear under her breath, dump her intended purchase down at the nearest opportunity and flounce out of the shop. However, this was the first piece of clothing she had wanted to buy in 10 years and so, contrary to her natural inclinations towards extreme impatience – she was a Londoner after all - she waited in line with gritted teeth while the next person ahead of her emptied their plastic carrier bag full of returned goods.

It seemed that although each customer had a cornucopia of items to bring back, none of them had bothered to bring back the one thing they really needed - their receipts. The process was clearly going to take some time. She continued to grit her teeth, play with her mobile phone - despite not having any signal - until finally it was her turn.

The cashier took the nightie, looked her up and down as if she were asking herself why someone like her would want to buy something so nice and then tried to persuade her to get a credit card. 'I live abroad,' she replied. She didn't but it shut up the shop assistant once and for all. She took £20 from her purse, which for the most part was bulging with receipts and vouchers that she would never use, and handed the note over to the cashier.

Once home, she was tempted to place her lovely new purchase where so many lovely new purchases of lingerie and nightwear had gone before – destined never to be worn. The lingerie graveyard that was her bottom drawer. There she kept all her sexy underwear in various sizes and colours, bought for that special romantic occasion which never came: sexy silk French knickers and matching tops, the odd sexy teddy from the early 90s.

She had once taken a set of black silk French knickers and matching top for a trip to the Lake District with a new boyfriend. It was their first romantic weekend away together and, as it transpired, their last. The new (and soon to be ex) boyfriend unilaterally decided to spend their first supposedly amorous night together engrossed in watching Match of the Day. In response, she unilaterally decided that to put the sexy lingerie on would be a complete waste of time. Thus, despite the best of intentions, the outfit never got an airing. The said items swiftly went back into her suitcase and from there straight back to their inevitable final resting place in the graveyard that was her lingerie drawer.

She wasn't quite sure why she insisted on keeping all these forlorn reminders of romantic wishful thinking from her past. It wasn't as if she could ever wear them, even in the unlikely event an opportunity arose where they would be required. Not only would her love life have to take a serious turn for the better, she'd also have to lose several stone or suddenly become the victim of a virulent wasting disease for them to fit.

She opened the drawer and looked at the various silken underwear before her - never worn and, more importantly, never taken off. She thought of all the almost-romances that marked her life, of the men she had spent years obsessing about to little avail and who, looking back, she now realised had, from the first, clearly not been that interested in her, if only she'd been prepared to admit it at the time. Her ability to delude herself, to read signs of hope where none existed and her dogged desire to be "understanding" in the face of general indifference belied her natural intelligence.

She then thought of the admirers she had either been indifferent to or whose overtures at the time she had been blithely unaware of. Yes, she conceded, for an intelligent woman she couldn't half be an idiot when it came to matters of the heart.

She remembered how her greatest fear as a young child was to end up like the mad, old lady she sometimes used to see on the No 16 bus. The woman, made up to the nines, but obviously lonely, would ride the No 16 bus all day, talking to strangers in the way that only truly lonely people do, talking non-stop, desperate to be in a conversation with another human being, with someone, anyone. Her sheer desperate need to converse would ensure that no one wanted to talk to her. People would do their very best to avoid the old lady, including her. Even as a small child she could sense the loneliness and desperation that engulfed this woman. She had prayed that she would not end up like her, but as she looked at the sea of multi-coloured silk in front of her, she reflected that her greatest fear was likely to come true. After all, her romantic life had not been that fantastic when she had been young and sexy. What were the chances now as a 50 something - albeit 5 lbs lighter than she had been 10 days before?

She thought of the men who she was still friends with and with whom at some point or other something might have happened, but in the end, nothing ever had. She conceded she had screwed up big time on at least a couple of occasions, when she had met men who, she realised in hindsight, would have been ideal for her. She had let these opportunities sail by, having no idea of how rare and valuable they were. 30 years on and there was definitely no going back.

Still sitting on her bed, clutching her new purchase, she thought of her friends who had found someone. Like a lot of women, she thought the majority of her friends could have done a lot better than the person they had ended up with. She was convinced they had settled. She couldn't tell them this of course. What would be the point? Even if they broke up with the said individual, she still couldn't say anything - just in case they got back with them. She'd learned that valuable lesson in her 20s when, elated at her then best friend breaking up with her long-term boyfriend, she had finally told her what she really thought of him. Needless to say, her friend got back with her boyfriend soon afterwards, told him what she had said about him and that was the end of that particular friendship.

She too had tried to settle in her early-30s. It turned out to be her longest lasting relationship. It had lasted all of 15 months. Yes, 15 months had been the longest a relationship of hers had ever lasted. It seemed a rather pathetically short amount of time given the years she had been alive. She had been well aware at the time that she was settling, but she felt empowered because deep down she didn't care. But it had come with a price and the price was that the relationship had numbed her soul. Then as soon as he suggested they move in together into his flat in South London, she promptly moved to Glasgow. Anyone who would rather move to a city over 400 miles away than move in with their boyfriend definitely had commitment issues. A month later they had split up, although that had been his idea.

When he'd suggested they break up, she'd nonchalantly replied: 'OK then'. The truth of the matter was she wasn't that bothered. She definitely didn't love him. She wasn't even sure she liked him. She suspected she had never liked him. What she had liked was the idea of having a boyfriend for once; that was what she had been more enamoured with rather than the reality of her relationship with him.

Having agreed that they should break up, she remembered putting down the phone and thinking she'd better cry. She was sure that was the correct response. She went into her bedroom and decided to cry for three songs. She reckoned that was the commensurate number of tunes for a 15-month relationship. She put on a tape of slow 80s love tunes – surely a safe choice – but half way through the first song she realised she couldn't be arsed.

She got up off the bed where she'd flung herself in a fit of supposed dramatic pique. She went into the kitchen and made herself a coffee and a cheese sandwich and turned on the portable TV. For the next couple of hours, she sat engrossed as she watched the omnibus episode of a particularly awful American soap opera. So awful that she couldn't help but watch it. It was like a bad car accident you drive past on the motorway. You know you shouldn't look but you just can't seem to tear yourself away.

Mulling all this over, she got up and went to put the nightie in the lingerie graveyard drawer. Then she remembered the one guy whom she had met, loved and lost and who – despite 20 years after their brief romance – she was still friends with. She thought how distraught she had been when the romance had died - though it had died a lot earlier than she had realised at the time; nine months before to be exact. When the penny finally dropped, she had felt as if she had been given everything she could ever want in a man only for it to be snatched away from her. She thought too about how he had never actually loved her despite finding her compelling and sexy. And then she remembered how needy she had been and, truthfully, she couldn't really blame him.

What were her options now? Men who thought that at her age and size she should just be grateful. She wasn't. Men who had clearly been with too many women with low self-esteem and as a result thought they could treat her accordingly. They couldn't. Married men who thought she would be up for being a bit on the side. No thanks. And recently an aging intellectual who had buckets full of charm, but the emotional make up of an insecure, spotty teenager.

The final straw was when he brought another woman along with him the last time they met up, and then seemed rather uncomfortable when she didn't seem elated at the prospect. Afterwards he had emailed her to apologise for behaving so badly and to let her know that the evening had been very unpleasant for him. In other words, he'd emailed her in order to apologise to himself. Strangely enough, they were no longer in touch.

She knew she had to do something to ensure that the nightie didn't end up suffering the same fate as all the sexy lingerie that had gone before it. Whilst pondering how exactly she was going to solve that little conundrum, she quickly undressed, slipped on the nightie and sat down on the edge of the bed. 'I'm not sure this counts,' she muttered to herself.

There comes a point in every woman's life when you become invisible to the opposite sex. Men stop paying attention to you, stop looking at you in that certain way, stop volunteering to do things for you or even stop noticing that you are there. When she was young, she hadn't appreciated the innate power she had as an attractive, young woman. Men had always been helpful and attentive. It happened so often that she assumed it was normal. It seemed so entirely natural that she didn't even question it. Then as the years passed it began to stop.

When it first started happening, she thought it was amusing. Then slowly her intrinsic power as an attractive woman dissipated almost completely and it threw her for six. The men she knew in her 20s still treated her as the sexy, young woman she had been. After all they still saw her, the real her, the her she still felt herself to be and not the middle-aged woman she'd become. However, in general, she had become transparent and this indifference ate away at her soul.

Yes, she had got older and the pounds had piled on, but she still believed herself to be the intelligent, witty and vivacious woman she had always considered herself to be. That hadn't changed, had it? The essential her was still there. Or had she been mistaken all that time? Maybe she hadn't been as interesting as she'd always imagined. Maybe people hadn't been attracted to what she perceived to be her quick wit and quick mind. Maybe people had simply indulged her because they found her attractive and shagable.

As she grew older, she noticed not only how invisible she was becoming but how middle-aged women seem to disappear from all aspects of society – from literature, from TV, from films, apparently not even allowed to read the news on TV. Of course, there were the odd exceptions where older women were allowed to make a fleeting appearance on screen: if they were personifying the interfering mother, the moaning ex-wife, the aged prostitute (invariably with a heart of gold), the doddering grand-mother, but in the main – unless they were Helen Mirren, Judi Dench or Maggie Smith - older women in TV and films were reduced to bit parts.

No wonder Sex and the City had been such a big success. It was one of the few programmes which featured women over 35 who weren't just someone's mother or embittered ex. Admittedly, her life was nothing like theirs. She never faced the horrendous quandary of having a limitless designer wardrobe or having to choose between two hot men such as Big and Aidan, but at least Carrie, Miranda, Charlotte and Samantha were more or less in the same age bracket as her.

While the programme had been running, she had always identified with Miranda, but what if she was more like Samantha in that deep down she never wanted to be in a relationship. Yes, she wanted love, she wanted sex, she wanted affection, but did she want to be in a relationship?

With the odd exception, whenever she visited her friends who were in long-term relationships, she tended to feel a sense of relief that she was not in their predicament. So much so that at times when she felt really down about her dogged single status, she would visit certain friends in long-term relationships just to cheer herself up, and remind herself that at least she had standards. After all, being alone in a relationship is a lot lonelier than being alone per se.

Yes, she had friends who were in happy relationships, but she pitied those whose partners seemed to delight in chipping away at their self-esteem, in belittling them, and to some extent controlling them. She knew she would never have been willing to pay that high a price for a relationship and children. Perhaps there were women out there who felt it was a price worth paying to nest: putting up with men who would day-by-day tear them down bit-by-bit. Needless to say, she rubbed such men up the wrong way simply by existing. Moreover, she would commit the worst sin a woman could make in their eyes – she refused to pander to their egos to make them feel better about themselves.

It dawned on her that all things considered, maybe her personality didn't suit being in a relationship. She knew that the idea of checking in with someone before doing anything appalled her even though she understood why couples did it. Even as a temp, she'd never ask permission before she did anything. She would simply tell her bosses what she was doing, whether it was to say she needed a day off or that she'd be late coming in. She reasoned that if you tell someone, rather than ask them, then they can't say no.

She recalled going to the cinema on a date with a guy who she had been totally enamoured with. Ironically, he was now openly gay. So much for her Gaydar. She couldn't believe her luck. She was spending the whole evening with him. They arrived at the cinema and, as it so happened, he wanted to see one film; she had wanted to see another. Without a moment's hesitation, she had blithely said: 'Well you go and see what you want to see and I'll go and see my film and then I'll meet you in the foyer afterwards.' Needless to say, there had been no second date.

She concluded that with that independence of mind (it sounded much better than selfishness or lack of consideration of others) maybe she wasn't cut out to be in a relationship after all. Even she would find it difficult to go out with someone like her and she understood where she was coming from! She was too old to start a family and she couldn't see any budding relationships happening anytime soon. What could she do with her life? Make the most of it, she decided. Read, travel, catch up with friends, write?

She had spent most of her life on hold – waiting for something to happen, that great work opportunity to appear, the love of her life to turn up, that one event which was going to turn her life around. And while she waited, most of her life had passed her by. Her ability to procrastinate and waste time was second to none. She would spend days, months, even years agonising over a decision and then always make the wrong choice. Surely, she could make the wrong choice a lot quicker?

'Christ,' the thought struck her. 'How much time have I wasted thinking about this bleeding nightie?' She went next door and got her Notebook. Returning to the bedroom, she crawled on to the bed and switched the Notebook on, banging her head against the headboard several times as it took an age to come to life. She thought to herself. 'Bloody start writing. Something. But write about what?' She looked down at her nightie and began to type.

THE VOID

The one thing you can't seem to escape as a performer is the void. It's always there, looming in the background, ready to swallow you up. At times it seems to dissipate, disappear and you think you've outrun it, buried it, lost it but it always comes back, threatening to swallow you up.

It often unfolds itself at the least expected moments, tripping you up when you should be at your happiest – after a great performance, after a great gig, after a career milestone. For days, months, years you've been telling yourself if only I get that role, play that club, get that gig, it – whatever it is – will be different: I'll be successful, I'll be respected by my peers, I'll get more work, I'll be rich. What you're really telling yourself is: I'll be happy.

Maybe you get that role, play that club, get that gig, maybe it goes well, maybe it doesn't, maybe it just goes OK, maybe it goes better than expected: whatever the outcome the void is still there and you're still not happy. If anything, the void is looming larger than before because it dawns on you yet again that that role, that club, that gig wasn't the panacea to your unhappiness, your loneliness, your fears. But you have no idea what else to do – dealing with what really makes you unhappy seems far more scary - so you carry on thinking that the next role you get, club you play, gig you smash will definitely make the difference.

A skilled comic has the power – and it is power - of ripping the room apart, all that laughter because of you, everyone hanging on your every word, your every facial expression, every well-judged pause, every ad lib that you've said a hundred times before; people coming up and telling you how amazing you were (and if you're a female comedian someone – and that someone is usually another woman - assuring you they found you funny even though they don't normally like female comedians) and then you're on the bus/tube/in the car homewards, often on your own, alone, and you've dissolved into nothing again. The people who thought you were wonderful, amazing, hilarious and were hanging on your every word just a mere half an hour ago have already started to forget you; you're simply a footnote in their night out; at most, you're hazily remembered as that funny comic they saw one night whose name they can't remember.

As a comic your art, your skill at making a room full of strangers enter into whatever world you create and getting them to laugh, is ephemeral. Gone as soon as you say the words. A comic is only as good as their last gig the saying goes and it's true. You can rip it one night and then have a room full of strangers stare at you in complete disdain the next. No one is bulletproof. Every comic has died and every comic knows that somewhere along the line – no matter how good they are, how skilled, how well-written their jokes, how good their banter, they will die again. The better you are, the more consistent you are, the less often it will happen but it will happen. Maybe it's that fear which keeps the bigger fears at bay.

It's ironic that people, who deep-down fear rejection, insist on putting themselves in a position where invariably they won't just be rejected by one person but rather by a whole room of people. In comedy, when you have a bad gig, it's not that the audience don't like your act, they invariably don't like YOU. It's not theatre; you can't hide behind the underwritten role, the out-of-depth director, the badly-written play: it's YOU, YOUR persona, YOUR words, confirming what you have always feared the most – that you're unlikeable and all those school bullies from years ago were right.

Then there is the rejection from promoters and bookers – some of whom would seem to know almost nothing about comedy but do enjoy the power they wield over their particular comedy empire. The constant knocking on doors which refuse to open even when you've done well all helps feed the void. After a while, your imagination starts working overtime and you begin to believe it's personal; you imagine that there is some big conspiracy to thwart your career as if bookers and promoters would seriously devote time and effort in stymieing you; but it's a far more tempting theory than the rather more prosaic if more likely reason that you're just another email in their inbox.

Fear of contacting promoters; fear of being rejected out-of-hand; of being ignored; passed over; the fear of silence, it all helps build that void. Perhaps most scarily of all, for someone who lives from their words is the void you feel when you come to write and you can't think of anything; you mind is a blank page so you try and fill that void by cleaning out the fridge, clearing out the shed, eating crap food, engaging in social media, watching some shite telly, anything to keep the void at bay, besides the one thing that might help solve it – to write.

When the void hits, it can make you realise what you've been running away from – love, affection, family, friends, sex, human companionship or perhaps more accurately the lack of them. For a job which exclusively has you in the centre of an ever-changing vortex of social situations, at heart the comic is always alone, and never more so when the void is about to envelop you.

Read on for the first three chapters of Maureen Younger's debut novel, *Fictional Lives*, available sometime in the future!

FICTIONAL LIVES

An absurdist anti-romantic love story cum detective mystery novel

by

Maureen Younger

"For books continue each other, in spite of our habit of judging them separately."

Virginia Woolf

"No book is ever closed...so long as we remain alive."

D.K. Broster

Fictional Lives refers to several literary personages but is hopefully written in such a way that no actual knowledge of any of these figures should impede the enjoyment of this novel. For anyone not tempted to Google further, here is all you need to know.

Lizzie Bennett	Heroine of Pride and Prejudice. Highly intelligent and quick-witted, she manages to snare the most eligible bachelor in Pride & Prejudice, despite possessing the very two qualities generally despised in a potential mate by many males of the species
Jane Bennett	Most beautiful and nicest of the Bennett sisters. She hooks only the second-most eligible bachelor to give hope to the fairer sex that despite all proof to the contrary brains will fare better than beauty
Mary Bennett	The swotty and boring sister
Lydia Bennett	The flighty sister

Darcy	Brooding hero who is initially misunderstood but deep down has a heart of gold. He also has the immense good fortune of being incredibly rich. In real life such brooding men are probably best to be avoided, as neither the heart of gold nor the money is a dead cert
Bingley	Darcy's best friend – rich and weak-willed
Wickham	Handsome, friendly, charming but poor, so obviously he's a player and a scoundrel
Mrs Bennett	Mother to the Bennett sisters and like many a mother before and since she is of constant embarrassment to her offspring
Mr Collins	Nincompoop member of the clergy
Aunt Catherine	Overbearing relative of Darcy
Georgina Darcy	Darcy's much younger sister, lovely and shy

Stefan Zweig

Brilliant Austrian writer who hardly anyone in Britain has heard of as sadly none of his works have been made into must-see Sunday television dramas for the BBC

Wolf Haas

Brilliant Austrian writer who has written a series of books featuring the hapless detective, Simon Brenner

Simon Brenner

Hapless Austrian detective

1

The Set Up

At the ripe old age of 50, or as she preferred to call it, 38, Maureen had decided she needed to earn a lot of money in the shortest amount of time possible; and the only feasible way she was going to do that was by writing an international bestseller. Unfortunately, she didn't know how and, more importantly, she didn't really have a story she wanted to tell. She felt like a character in a novel. Unfortunately for Maureen, she felt like one of those characters who chose the wrong path in the first half of the novel only to live a lifetime of regret in the final chapters.

Then she remembered the adage: write what you know. Well, she knew about herself. She found herself fascinating, but even Maureen wasn't convinced that alone had the makings of an international bestseller. Write the type of book you like to read. She liked reading classical German and Austrian literature. And although at a push she might be able to change her nationality, she was pretty certain she wouldn't be able to travel back in time. Maureen was stuck.

'At least I'm not bitter,' she mused. 'After all, it could be worse. At least my life isn't like a Thomas Hardy novel.'

Then the thought struck her. Although it was far too late to rewrite her story in real life, she could rewrite her story in fiction. Borrow a plot already written, and preferably one with a happy ending, if she was going to be the main character; a story that was so well known that the characters would spring from the page, irrelevant of any writing ability she might or might not possess. Ideally with a female heroine whom readers could relate to and kid themselves they resembled and with a sexy hero to boot. A happy ending meant that Wuthering Heights was out of the running as were quite a few heroines from French classical literature such as Nana, Thérèse Raquin or Madame Bovary. Neither prostitution, murder nor infidelity followed by suicide fitted Maureen's idea of how her life might pan out, even if it were only on paper.

Maureen conceded that she often had problems identifying with various heroines in books and films. They didn't seem to think or act like she did. Even more annoyingly, they were often a hell of a lot younger than she was too.

Films in particular were a problem. There are those films which begin with the woman hating the hero, but nevertheless they end up with her falling madly and deeply in love with him. As a general rule, if Maureen took an initial dislike to a bloke, she still hated him come what may. Then there are the films which have Maureen rolling her eyes in disbelief; secretly wanting to smash something through the screen.

She thought of the classic French movie Belle de Jour. Here you had one of the most beautiful women ever seen on screen, Catherine Deneuve, portraying a woman who, having intimacy problems with her husband, decides to become a prostitute. Maureen appreciated Catherine was French, but surely even French women did what British women do when they find themselves in such a predicament – get pissed and fantasise about somebody else. More unbelievably, Catherine then nips down to her local brothel - luckily for her she just happens to know where it is - and asks for a job; whereupon the Madame immediately agrees to hire her despite Catherine pointing out she can only work between 2-5 in the afternoon. Hours, Maureen suspected, which weren't peak time for prostitution, even in France.

Then there were the horror films such as the one where the heroine decides to spend her holiday in some deserted shack in the middle of some god-forsaken wood, where lo and behold the local, psychotic axe murderer just happens to be on the loose. On hearing a noise outside, the heroine decides to inspect what's happening, but only once she has judiciously stripped down to her undies; as presumably she can see better when attired only in her bra and knickers.

Even in films Maureen liked there would often be moments when their portrayal of the heroine would set her teeth on edge. Maureen recalled a film she loved where the heroine insists on wearing massive, unflattering, old-school glasses. Later on in the movie, the hero asks her: Do you need those glasses? No, our heroine replies and whips them off. Maureen couldn't help wondering why the hell, if that were the case, she had been wearing them in the first place!

Then there are those idealised saintly heroines. They drove Maureen up the wall such as Mademoiselle Manette in A Tale of Two Cities. Her character was so annoyingly perfect Maureen would have been quite prepared to guillotine the woman herself. It had put her off reading Dickens for 10 whole years, until she had the good fortune to come across Great Expectations in an otherwise miserable year spent at drama school being persistently told she had no talent.

But then there was always an Austen novel. These are stories where the main conceit is that intelligent men are attracted to intelligent women with a mind of their own. Maureen secretly suspected that those few intelligent men who were attracted to strong, intelligent women with a mind of their own were – for the most part - gay. All things considered, as there didn't seem to be that many straight men that fitted the bill in the 21st century, she was sceptical as to how many would have existed over 200 years earlier, but she was willing to put her scepticism aside and go for it.

*   *   *

It is a truth universally acknowledged that a single man in possession of a good fortune must be in want of a wife. Well, the strapline on the latest issue of the tattered women's magazine Maureen was glancing at didn't say that, but it was kind of the gist. Anyway, it's the 21st century and no one speaks like that anymore. What the strapline actually said was: 10 Rules on How to Hook 10 of Hollywood's Hottest Hunks.

'You're seriously not going to read that article?' Maureen asked, shaking her head at her closest friend, Sue, while her hallmark throaty laugh erupted across the tube carriage.

Sue and Maureen had become best friends via a mutual friend who neither were in touch with anymore. Like many women they had the ability to create intense and intimate friendships with others of their sex, then fall out with them over something or other and then refuse to have anything more to do with them ever again. This is what had happened with both of them at different times with said mutual friend.

Sue was 10 years younger than Maureen and several stone lighter. Hailing from Coventry, both her parents had been of an artistic bent, but the practicalities of life and four children had forced them to take mundane jobs, her father in a car plant, her mother helping out in a cousin's nearby shop. Like her parents, Sue had a soft spot for the arts and dreamt of becoming an actor. Unable to overcome her natural timidity and self-doubt, she hovered around the edges, working in PR for various theatre companies.

Sue had an inimitable style all of her own. It was half hippy, half jumble sale chic, but no matter what she wore, Sue always made it seem as if she were dressed in the height of fashion. Every outfit topped by the obligatory peaked cap, always placed at an angle over her long, straight black hair. The overall effect was helped in no small part by her well-proportioned figure and pretty face; her only concessions to make up being a dash of lip gloss, lashings of mascara and copious amounts of eyeliner setting off her jet-black eyes.

Maureen invariably dressed in cocktail dresses, heels and fishnet tights (the latter less for their possible sex appeal more for reasons of thrift – they lasted longer and could be sewn up if push came to shove), and had wild, unruly hair which she rarely bothered combing. While Maureen could easily be located in any restaurant or bar by dint of her loud, throaty laugh, Sue was quieter and had a laugh that all comics instinctively hate: an ability to giggle without emitting any sound whatsoever.

Both the women had been avidly pretending to be engrossed in the magazine for the last five minutes, ever since an evidently pregnant woman had been standing in their direct eye line; and like everyone else lucky enough to grab a seat on the packed London tube train, they were determined not to see either her or her protruding stomach.

'What's wrong with having a read? Who knows? We might end up hooking one of the hunks. You never know,' Sue replied.

'I think we do know,' Maureen reassured her in a knowing voice

'You certain you don't want to have a look? Ryan Gosling and George Clooney are two of the hunks!' Sue said encouragingly, wafting the relevant page in front of Maureen to tempt her further.

'How old is that magazine?' Maureen snapped, 'Not to put a damper on things, but I'm guessing one of the rules is you have to live in Hollywood rather than East London, and secondly, you need to be 20 years younger than the hunk in question. Personally, I'm not sure how many 70-year old hunks there are out there. I can't believe you buy that crap.'

'Oh, I didn't buy it. I borrowed it from the doctor's waiting room.'

'Borrowed as in stolen I'm presuming,' said Maureen, raising an eyebrow. 'Well, I suppose there has to be some perks to being an inveterate hypochondriac.'

Sue blushed.

'No, honestly, Maureen, the magazine looks dead interesting. There's also a really great article about how to please your boyfriend in bed.'

'You don't say. What use is that to you? Or to me for that matter? We've both been single for zonks. Anyway, wouldn't it make more sense, in the unlikely event we should finally find ourselves with a boyfriend, to simply ask *him* instead? Personally, I find blow jobs are a tried and trusted method.'

Sue blushed more deeply, nervously looking around the packed compartment, and secretly wishing, and not for the first time, that Maureen's voice wasn't so commanding or her laugh so distinctive.

'To be honest,' Maureen was on a roll now and determined to ignore Sue's demeanour or those of her fellow travellers for that matter, most of whom seemed to have decided their conversation had taken a turn for the better and was of general import, 'I find it hard to believe, Sue, you have so much difficulty finding a boyfriend in the first place.'

Her conclusion seemed to arouse general agreement from all their fellow passengers, now keenly listening in.

'Well, I'm doing what I can,' Sue replied plaintively, 'I'm even giving internet dating a go.' She leaned into Maureen's shoulder and whispered rather conspiratorially into Maureen's left ear. 'Didn't you try it once?'

'Yes,' Maureen bellowed through another throaty laugh. 'But I soon gave it up as a bad lot.'

'Why?' Sue enquired wide-eyed and intrigued.

'Well, it turns out that at my age you end up being a babe magnet for either 70-year olds or 26-year-old Tunisians presumably on the hunt for a visa. Neither group particularly appeal if I'm brutally honest.'

'Wouldn't you like to be with somebody?'

'In theory, yes. But I'd rather be on my own than be in a relationship with a twat,' said Maureen, the heavy emphasis on the final T giving rise to at least one raised eyebrow amongst their fellow commuters.

'Fair enough,' Sue sighed 'but I'm feeling a bit down about this singleton life.'

'Oh, you should do what I always do whenever I feel down about being single.'

'What's that?' Sue enquired hopefully.

'Stay with friends in a long-term relationship. It doesn't half cheer you up. You look at your mate and it suddenly hits you why you're single. Unlike her, you've got standards. How's the internet dating going for you then?'

Sue again whispered conspiratorially in Maureen's ear, 'Can you believe one guy asked me to send, you know,' Sue paused for a second, 'you know. Photos of myself.'

'What kind of photos?'

'You know,' Sue looked around the tube carriage, evidently mortified. She caught Maureen's eye and mouthed, 'You know, when you've got nothing on.'

'Ah, those kinds of photos.' Maureen bellowed, her laugh ringing out through the tube carriage. 'You should do what I did when someone asked me to do that.'

'What was that?'

'Acted dumb. Just sent him loads of photos of me in different tops.'

*   *   *

Thirty minutes later, Sue and Maureen stood at the front path to the overpriced flat they had bought together in East London. In common with most of the street, it resembled less a front path and more of an It's a Knockout obstacle course, the theme of which was how many plastic bins can one council fit onto the smallest slither of land possible. They had given up trying to close the front gate years ago when it had been ordained, from up on high, that along with the two grey bins and the green bin for recycling, they now needed a brown bin for their garden waste. As neither they nor their upstairs neighbours did any gardening, so by extension never had any gardening waste, its only real use had been to hem in the front gate and block the entry to the path.

They squeezed past the bins, trying not to land in the muddy patch masquerading as a garden to their left. As usual, neither of the women had their keys to hand. Maureen sighed and started to empty the contents of her capacious handbag onto the lid of one of the grey bins. (It turned out they did have their uses after all). It was times like these that Maureen wished she kept her front door keys in the side pocket of her handbag where she kept meaning to put them.

In films and on TV, women always seemed to be able to locate immediately the precise thing they were looking for in their handbags. There could only be one sensible conclusion for this egregious misrepresentation of reality. Most scriptwriters must be men with evidently little understanding of the black hole quality that most women's handbags seemed to acquire. She was still rooting through her own handbag's contents, when suddenly the front door swung open as if by magic. In the doorway stood Maureen's mum, Mrs B.

Maureen's mum didn't live with them, but acted like an unofficial squatter. She had an uncanny knack of knowing when the flat would be empty and then using the spare keys to let herself in. Her ability not to take a hint was legendary as was her temper.

Mrs B.'s intransigence had reached its zenith when she had turned up one morning at 8:00 am. Any time Mrs B. suspected Maureen to be in – and first thing in the morning was a pretty safe bet - she always rang the doorbell first. She claimed she did this out of politeness. Maureen guessed it was more out of a well-founded fear that Maureen might take her keys away otherwise. That morning a more dishevelled than usual Maureen answered the door.

Unbeknownst to Mrs B, at the time, Maureen had been enjoying a fling with a man 17 years her junior and was taking full and repeated advantage of the situation. It was all very empowering. He was gorgeous, the sex was off the scale and as he was so much younger than her, Maureen had no illusions about their fling turning into a relationship. At one fell stroke, all insecurities were gone and instead of worrying about a possible future Maureen was enjoying the present. Until Mrs B. rang the doorbell.

Maureen looked aghast at her mother standing on the doorstep.

'Go get a newspaper,' she suggested, playing for time.

'I've got a newspaper,' her mum waved a copy of The Metro as irrefutable proof.

'Go get another one,' Maureen snapped abruptly and slammed the door, returning to her young lover in bed.

Five minutes later the doorbell rang out again. Mrs B. was now standing with a copy of the Daily Mail in her hands, newly purchased from the corner shop. It was clear that Mrs B. was here to stay, and Maureen's enjoyable morning ritual with lover boy would have to be postponed. Maureen didn't know how, but her mum always seemed to turn up at just the wrong moment.

Her mother's temper was best illustrated by an episode that occurred on the world tour she embarked on following her retirement. Mrs B. had decided to travel the world, ostensibly to see the sights, but as an inveterate chain smoker had mainly concentrated on countries where you could buy cheap fags.

Mrs B. was in Moscow. A foolish local girl, spotting what seemed to be an elderly woman in the crowd, mistakenly took Mrs B. for an easy target, clearly unaware that she was Scottish. The would-be assailant grabbed Mrs B.'s purse. Mrs B. responded by grabbing the mugger by the throat, and then proceeded, rather expertly, to throttle the living daylights out of her. Without further ado, Mrs B. threw her assailant to the ground, grabbed back her purse and finished by repeatedly calling the now traumatised attacker a cunt, in a Scottish accent which had become all the thicker with every pulsating moment of Mrs B.'s sturdy defence of her property. The girl fled, presumably to later find refuge in some psychiatric unit which dealt with survivors suffering from acute PTSD.

Mrs B. was one of those women who had come of age in the 1950s. From working-class stock, the only options open to women such as her in those days were marriage or a dead-end job or both. In 1950s Dundee that meant work as a weaver in a jute mill. Mrs B. had finally escaped mill life by marrying Maureen's dad and persuading him they should move to London.

Like many a woman of her generation she was jealous of the opportunities her own daughter had enjoyed and was frustrated by her own life of menial jobs and its dearth of opportunities. She saw in her daughter's life all the potential she could have had in her own had she been born but a few decades later. She was known as Mrs B., as that had been her father-in-law's nickname for her, and it had somehow stuck. It was widely assumed among Maureen's Scottish relatives that the B stood for besom.

Mrs B. was incredibly lonely. She had separated from Maureen's father 30 years ago and had since fallen out, one by one, with a now ever diminishing circle of friends. Consequently, she made the most of any opportunity to talk to another human being, whether they were listening to her or not. Before Maureen could scrape her belongings back into her handbag, Mrs B. let Maureen and Sue know the latest gossip.

'You won't believe who's moved into the area,' she said in a thicker Scottish accent than usual. Maureen noticed, and not for the first time, that when her mum got angry, drunk or excited, her accent would inevitably become more Scottish circa 1950s. At times, it was like having a conversation with Ma Broon.

'Erm, won't we?' Sue asked.

'Two blokes.'

'Gay!' Maureen muttered to herself.

'Well,' Mrs B. continued, ignoring her daughter's contribution to the conversation, 'as luck would have it, I happened to be passing as this Charlie guy was moving in across the road.'

'That was handy,' Maureen interrupted and emitted a throaty chuckle.

This news confirmed once more Maureen's belief in her mother's unnatural skill at being in the right place at exactly the time when it was most inconvenient to everyone else concerned.

'I was chatting to Charlie Bingley, I think that's what he said his name was, he's the one who has bought the downstairs flat across the road, number 46, and he happened to mention that we'll probably see a lot of him and his best mate, as his mate has just bought a house nearby in Walthamstow village.'

The last two words were enunciated with the awe due to it by any reasonable soul who had kept an eye on house prices recently. Maureen mused that she had been right all along. Walthamstow was going upmarket. It wouldn't be long now before all the greasy spoons would be upgrading, along with their prices as they morphed into cafes. Next thing they would be serving artisan wholemeal soda bread with bleeding oil instead of good old-fashioned white sliced bread and butter. This news of the two guys moving in confirmed one of Maureen's greatest fears - Walthamstow was heading the way of Balham.

Maureen had to admit that, for once, Mrs B. had some newsworthy information. Two guys moving into the area, apparently single and yet still able to buy property in London. All three women knew what this meant. They had to find out as soon as possible if the men were gay or not, and in the unlikely event that they were straight, if they were single.

2

Machinations

Later that afternoon, and in the hope of spotting their new neighbour, Sue and Maureen stood in their cramped front room looking out of the window, their view partially blocked by an old-fashioned white and blue Volkswagen campervan, with its colourful curtains drawn. It seemed to have taken root overnight outside their house.

'That campervan is a pain,' Maureen sighed. 'Wonder whose it is? It can't belong to him next door, surely?'

'Doubt it. It's got foreign number plates.'

'Really? I hadn't noticed.'

'I only noticed because the plate starts with my initials – ST.'

'ST? Where's that from then?' Maureen asked.

'No idea. Just spotted the two initials at the start and thought that it can't be British. I wish it would move though. I can hardly see a thing. How the hell are we going to engineer meeting this Charlie bloke?' Sue craned her neck around Maureen's mass of hair to get a better view of No. 46.

'God knows!' Maureen answered and let out a heartfelt sigh. 'I know in Pride and Prejudice women got to socialise with men at Assembly Balls. Not sure there are that many Assembly Balls in East London anymore, even in Walthamstow Village.'

'I've an idea. Maybe we could have an old-fashioned house party and invite all the neighbours.'

'Knowing our luck,' Maureen snorted, making full use of her tendency to always see the negative in life, 'mum will turn up and the guys won't. Either that or the guys will bring their boyfriends along.'

Sue looked crestfallen.

'Anyway,' Maureen continued blithely, 'when was the last time you heard of anyone having a house party? 1986? In those good old days before Tinder, before the invention of apps and mobile phones and Facebook, when everyone had physically met all their friends. Those halcyon days when you met someone in real life before you decided whether you wanted to sleep with them or not. My gawd, it all seems so quaint now.

'Those long gone days when you'd arrive at a party and walk into someone's kitchen or living room, and instead of checking out their virtual, photo-shopped images online, you could see them in the flesh and check out each individual in turn and, in your head, go, no, no, no, no, yes, and then, if you're British, spend the rest of the evening doggedly ignoring the only viable prospect in the room while steadily getting more and more pissed, and then finish off the evening by wondering why in heaven's name they hadn't asked you out.'

'You're right, it was so much easier back then,' Sue concluded ruefully.

Maureen wasn't convinced Sue had understood the point she was making. Her suspicion was soon confirmed as a large grin crossed

Sue's face. 'Well, I think we should go for it. We can invite all the neighbours.' She sounded genuinely excited at the prospect.

'These would be the same people we have studiously tried to avoid speaking to since we moved in here.'

Sue refused to be put off track.

'No, the same people YOU have been studiously trying to ignore since we moved in here. I say let's invite them over. We can lay on a small buffet. What harm can it do?'

'Have you tasted my cooking?' Maureen responded with a withering glance.

'I'll do the cooking,' Sue persisted.

Maureen gave up. 'OK but as long as there is some proper 1970s fare – cheese and pineapple, sausage rolls that kind of thing. No bloody canapés.'

'You're on.'

'But before we go mad at Iceland,' Maureen replied, 'have you ever considered that every woman always thinks when reading Pride and Prejudice that she is Lizzie Bennett. No one reads it and thinks well, I'm definitely Kitty. In my experience, far too many women are less Lizzie Bennett more Charlotte Lucas. You know, smart, intelligent women who for some reason or other choose to nest with complete idiots.

'To be fair, in the novel, Charlotte Lucas has an excuse for marrying Mr Collins. Financial necessity. But what's the excuse nowadays? But I bet even all those modern Charlottes are still convinced they are Lizzie Bennett and wondering why the idiot they are with is nothing like Darcy. Because we always make that mistake, don't you think when we identify with a novel, of seeing ourselves as the heroine of the story? No one ever reads a book and thinks for one single minute that they're the sidekick or one of the peripheral characters – you know the one who everyone feels sorry for or forgets they're even in the novel and then they suddenly appear and you're never quite sure what purpose they serve.'

Both friends glanced over at their friend Jenny, who had called in 10 minutes earlier, and was sitting in a corner thumbing through Tinder.

'I mean I'm pretty sure I'm Lizzie…,' Maureen was about to hold forth when she could sense a pout coming on around the lips of her closest friend. 'But let's face it, I spend most of my time reading German and Austrian literature and checking the translations of subtitles in German and French movies against what the people are saying in the film.'

'You do that?' interjected Jenny, tearing herself away for a minute from her smart phone's screen.

'Might do,' Maureen replied. 'That's not the point. With attributes like that what if I'm the boring sister, Mary and not the heroine, Lizzie.'

'Who am I?' Sue pleaded.

'Well, I'd say Jane,' Maureen said reassuringly. 'The pretty one.'

'What about me?' Jenny interjected once more.

'Lydia!' Maureen and Sue replied in unison.

*   *   *

'OK there's another problem with this Pride and Prejudice malarkey,' Maureen mused.

'I think using the word malarkey might possibly be one of them. It isn't very 19th century, is it?' noted Jenny who was beginning to become rather annoying.

'Oh no, I don't mind using the plot – it's a good one after all – but I'm not going to even try and approximate the language or the period setting.'

'Why's that?' asked Jenny again. Maureen was beginning to feel that for a peripheral character Jenny had far too much to say for herself.

'Too much research.'

'So, sheer laziness then? I thought you liked history?'

Maureen was starting to have serious doubts about introducing Jenny into the literary proceedings for the mere sake of what was supposedly to be a one-off joke on peripheral characters.

'No, not exactly,' Maureen lied.

Fortunately, for Maureen, she was a quick thinker, so she continued in a much more adamant vein. 'If I wrote a period piece, someone like me would be working 15-hour days as somebody's servant; if I was lucky! That's what people forget when they bang on about how romantic that period was. Possibly, if you were fortunate enough to be born a lady, but even then, these women had few rights, couldn't hang on to their own property once they were married, had no rights even over their own children and they were the fortunate ones! People like me would have been working all the hours God sends for sod all money, and if some young master took a fancy to me, I could do sod all about it. It would be assumed I'd led him on in the first place and I'd be the one out on her ear, with no references and no hope of another job. With no other choices presumably but to beg, steal or whore.'

'Well, I suppose if you put it like that,' Jenny conceded.

'No, I'm mainly interested in the plot of Pride and Prejudice and this is where we have our next major problem. Darcy and Lizzie, Bingley and Jane finally get together when Lizzie realises all that Darcy has done to save Lydia from herself and rescue the family from shame and ignominy. Yes?'

'Ignominy, now that's more like it,' said Jenny approvingly and turned her attention back to Tinder. Maureen looked over at the phone's screen. If that was some bloke's image, it clearly wasn't his nose.

'Well?' Sue said uncertain as to the point Maureen was trying to make.

'Well, firstly none of us have annoying younger sisters who can embarrass us. Secondly, even if we did, in this day and age who cares if someone's younger sister is living-in-sin with somebody?'

'I see what you mean.'

'I mean OK, maybe in some cultures. But definitely not in my family nor in those of any of our mates. Take Sukh. From an arty, Sikh family who doesn't give a damn that she dates white guys. Where are stereotypes when you need them? Could you imagine having her as a character and not wrapping her up in some burning social issue of the day? Bleeding Nora. That would annoy the hell out of some of those white, middle-class critics, believe you me.'

'You think?'

'Definitely. Don't you remember when we went to see that play in Kilburn where most of the characters were Asian?'

Sue looked blankly at Maureen.

'Sue, you were doing the PR for it. I can't remember the name of it myself. No reflection on your PR skills, by the way, Sue. It was a comedy, very enjoyable in fact. Remember how the white critics loathed it. Asian cast and no arranged marriages, no brute of a father. I don't think they could get their head around a play featuring Asian characters that just told a story, was funny and wasn't replete with issues. I suppose it felt a bit like they'd been cheated, like watching a Christmas episode of EastEnders without the misery.'

3

Old Flames Never Die

Just then the doorbell rang. Maureen sallied to the door and opened it. Standing in front of her was her first great love.

'Walter!'

Walter and Maureen stared at each other, neither of their faces revealing the inner turmoil that they were both feeling. Maureen didn't know whether to hug him or shut the door in his face. Walter couldn't decide if what he was feeling was trepidation or some perverse form of excitement.

A former policeman, Walter had been in some tense situations, but nevertheless he had needed to steel himself, primarily with a bottle or two of beer, before ringing the doorbell; it felt like he was opening up a Pandora's Box to both the past, and possibly the present. He was a simple man, with simple tastes; he would have preferred to have spent his life sitting in the house he'd inherited from his parents in his little Styrian village, reading book upon book. Instead, against his nature and inclination, out of some perverse sense of – he wasn't sure what it was exactly – he had joined the police. Everyone who knew him had been taken aback. Surely working in an office would suit this careful, considerate, bookish man better? As if to emphasise his academic and thoughtful nature, Walter wore metal-rimmed glasses which he seemed to be for ever pushing back up his nose and dressed in a fashion which could be best described as staid.

But precisely because he didn't think he would enjoy working as a policeman, he felt it was the right job for him. Why do something you enjoy? What if it went wrong? Then what? As it turned out, his stolid manner had proved quite effective, much to the surprise of both his colleagues and, not least, himself.

Walking back into Maureen's life was frightening enough, but being in London made him feel off-kilter and added to his anxiety. To him Vienna was a metropolis; too many people, too much traffic, too polluted. Having arrived in Old London Town, he realised why Maureen had laughed at his complaints of 1980s Vienna. Vienna was bad enough, but he couldn't understand how anyone could live in London. Making his way through the city streets, avoiding the hordes of people walking with their heads down, scrolling through the screens on their phones, being summarily shouted at by furious Londoners for committing the apparently heinous crime of standing on the left-hand side of the escalator, then trying to fight for space on a packed tube train during rush hour, had reminded him that Maureen and he were from two different worlds. They were preordained always to look at things from opposite angles.

Then there was all the drama of their past. He'd hurt her. He had never intended to, but he had kept on hurting her because he couldn't let go. He had never wanted to hurt anyone, but she had always demanded more than he could give her and she never seemed to understand that basic truth. Their last parting had been tense to say the least. He could still remember her pent up fury, her tears. He hoped against hope that time had mellowed her. From the look on her face, he wasn't convinced it had.

On hearing Maureen shout out the name of the guy whose actions, or more precisely inactions, Sue had been forced to spend many an hour with Maureen analysing and commenting on despite never having met him, Sue's voice promptly echoed down the hall, 'Hang on a minute. In what part of Pride and Prejudice does an Austrian appear?'

Maureen looked over her shoulder and shouted back, 'Well, I thought I'd mix it up a bit and in homage to Wolf Haas add in an Austrian detective.'

It was nonsense of course. It had nothing to do with Wolf Haas but Maureen guessed that as soon as she mentioned anything to do with Austrian literature, Sue would be keen to change the subject; and for once Maureen was keen to change subjects. She always was when she sensed she might have to discuss her emotions.

'Wolf? I thought you said Walter just now.'

Turning to Walter for a brief second, Maureen mouthed the words, 'Moment, Schatzi,' while she closed the front door on him and turned towards her inquisitor.

'Yes, he's called Walter,' Maureen said, pointing at the door behind her, and thinking on her feet once more, she added, 'Wolf Haas is a novelist. A very successful, Austrian author in fact. He's written a series of detective novels featuring a certain private detective, Simon Brenner. Great books. I was so disappointed when I'd finished reading them all. Suddenly, I knew how all those Sherlock Holmes fans must have felt when Conan Doyle tried to get rid of Holmes by sending him over the Reichenbach Falls. I was so desperate to read some more

Haas I even read his novel about motorcar racing which, strangely enough, despite its setting, I still enjoyed. Haas is very Austrian, you know,' – clearly Sue didn't – 'funny, keen sense of the absurd, macabre. Conversational in style. Although admittedly the conversational-in-style bit isn't Austrian per se.'

Sue continued to look nonplussed though Maureen suspected the look was veering more towards sheer indifference.

'Mind you, I'm not sure how well-known Haas is in the UK.'

Maureen paused for a second, glanced at the door and then back at Sue.

'Though I suppose that could be a major advantage all things considered.'

'So, this guy is like this fictional detective, Simon Brenner?'

'Hell no. He's Austrian and he's hapless but that's about it.'

'So, he's based on the real Walter?'

'No, not really.'

'Really? He's not based on you know who? Well, who then?'

'Well, he is, obviously, but I have to say that just in case you know who reads this.'

'Is that likely?'

'Let's hope not!'

And with that in mind, Maureen opened the door and invited Walter Trotta inside. Sue was intrigued to finally meet Walter, but if truth be told she was disappointed. Of average height, with his thinning sandy blond hair, his glasses and sensible dress sense, Sue thought he looked less like a detective and more like a progressive teacher of Religious Education. He had a warm smile and looked nice, one of the worst adjectives a woman can bestow on a man. It was clear he was still enamoured with Maureen as he couldn't seem to take his eyes off her. A fact Maureen seemed oblivious to.

As Sue well knew, Walter had been the great love of Maureen's life in her youth. She had met him in the mid-1980s when she had gone to Vienna to study German. Arriving in Austria, Maureen soon realised the one major flaw in her grand, linguistic plan. Austrians speak their own version of German. To paraphrase George Bernard Shaw: Germany and Austria are two countries separated by a common language.

Maureen had no idea of this. She was ignorant of anything across from the English Channel in Europe. Like most Brits, Maureen clung steadfastly to the unique British theory that Britain wasn't in Europe per se despite its geographical location, but an entity entirely of its own. It was only when she arrived in Vienna after a tedious 24-hour train journey, that the linguistic challenge she faced became apparent. She had arrived safely enough, but her two very large suitcases hadn't. (Maureen had only learnt to pack lightly with the advent of budget airlines). Needless to say, it came as a bit of a shock when, enquiring about her missing suitcases at Vienna's West Station, she found the only person who spoke 'proper' German was her.

However, unlike most British students who went abroad to learn German and then spent their whole time there determinedly speaking English with their British mates, Maureen had only had Austrian friends. As a result, even 30 years later Maureen still spoke German with a definite Austrian twang.

So strong was her Austrian accent that on one occasion when she was translating for an English friend at a party in Berlin, a Berliner, hearing the Viennese lilt and assuming she was Austrian, reassured her that her English wasn't *too* bad. Maureen chivalrously thanked him whereupon he pointed out that despite her fluency, her English grammar was shit. Maureen replied that of course her grammar was shit. She was British. That was how you could tell she was a native English speaker: Britain being one of the few countries in Europe back then where the teaching of grammar had largely been considered irrelevant.

While a student, Maureen had ended up sharing a flat in central Vienna having answered an advertisement from someone who was looking to share with either a Frenchwoman or a Spaniard. Maureen was neither, but as she was foreign, she concluded it was more or less the same thing, and duly rang up and got the flat. Opposite her lived three guys whose front door didn't lock properly. This being 1980s Vienna it wasn't much of a security issue. It also had the advantage that Maureen and her flatmate could walk into the flat whenever they liked by flipping up the lock, and therefore tended to regard the boys' front room/kitchen as an extension of their own flat. As the men could cook better than them and were extremely good company, not surprisingly they ended up spending more time in the boys' flat than their own.

For some reason, out of the three, she and Walter clicked, though on paper they seemed a most unlikely pairing. At the time he had a girlfriend who, it is fair to say, nobody liked including - one suspected - Walter. As for Maureen and Walter, it had proved to be an on-off affair that had lasted for several years with the greater emphasis on *off* and a lot of attendant heartache for Maureen.

Faced with seeing her former great love for the first time in thirty years, Maureen did what any sane British person would do in her position; she went straight to the kitchen and switched the kettle on. Several minutes later Walter Trotta grimaced in utter disdain as Maureen stirred a mug of instant coffee. He was surprised that she had made such an elementary mistake when serving a hot beverage to an Austrian. Whereas coffee culture had been raised to an art form in Austria, Walter concluded, while looking at his cuppa, that in Britain it had been plunged to its lowest common denominator. He graciously accepted the proffered mug, placed it on the kitchen table in front of him and chose to politely forget about it.

'Why are you here?' Maureen asked, not quite believing that after all these years Walter was standing in her kitchen.

He grinned. 'To see you.'

'After 30 years?' Maureen's throaty laugh echoed cynically around the kitchen.

That was slow even by Austrian standards. Mind you, if it had taken Walter Trotta 30 years to get around to seeing her, then the Austrian police force was even less on the ball than their public transportation system. A system – as in many aspects of Austrian life

– which exemplified the nation's dedication to absurdity. When Maureen had lived in Vienna there had been three underground lines numbered 1, 2 and 4. Last time she was there, there were five, numbered 1, 2, 3, 4 and 6. That was Austria.

'To see me?' Maureen repeated incredulously. 'What's the real reason? Why are you really here?' She was pragmatic if nothing else.

'Well, as it happens, I'm also on the hunt for a murdering catholic priest, Father B.'

'And?'

'Well, admittedly that's the main reason why I'm here, but I always did want to see you again.'

'And it took a murdering catholic priest to set the wheels in motion? I mean we're not even friends on Facebook, and I'm friends with people on there I don't even know. What did you say this murdering priest's name was?'

'Father B. B as in the letter B.'

Despite his fluent English, Walter opted for the German pronunciation of the letter. Maureen nodded her head in agreement while Sue looked confused.

'What letter is bay?' Sue asked.

'He means bee as in the letter B,' Maureen explained.

'He definitely said bay,' Sue insisted.

'Yes,' Maureen replied, trying not to sound too exasperated, 'the letter B sounds like bee in English, but when pronounced in German to an English ear it sounds like bay. OK?' Maureen turned to Walter. 'What does the initial stand for anyway?'

'I don't know. I don't know his name. I just know the initial and the fact he has a rather distinguishing mark.'

'What? A mole in the shape of a crucifix? He's bald? Has a limp?' Maureen helpfully suggested.

'No, he has two golden hands.'

'Wasn't that a Bond villain?' Sue interrupted.

'No,' Maureen replied, 'that was Goldfinger. Two golden hands,' Maureen repeated in disbelief. 'What, he has two hands made of gold? They must weigh a ton. How would that be possible?'

'They must have cost him a fortune,' Sue chipped in, "I wanted to buy some new gold earrings the other day. You won't believe how much they wanted to charge.'

Both Walter and Maureen stared at Sue for a second or two then Maureen decided to ask a far more pertinent question.

'What's he done then?'

'He strangles his victims. It's not a pretty sight. We believe he's behind a series of strangulations in Styria. You might have heard of him – The Styrian Strangler?'

'Well, no, it hasn't made the news over here I'm afraid, though it's nice alliteration, at least in English.'

'Thanks. We have reliable information that leads us to believe he's come to London and I was wondering if you could help. You see I'm not here officially. I've had to leave the police but...'

'So that's why you're here. You'd like me to help you track down a murdering catholic priest with metal hands.'

'Yes,' Walter looked lovingly in Maureen's eyes and she paused for a moment in reverie.

'Not a hope in hell!'

*   *   *

Maureen, Sue and Walter were bent over the kitchen table looking at a piece of paper laid out in front of them. Walter had easily managed to overcome Maureen's refusal to help by tempting her with the one thing he knew she couldn't resist apart from chocolate– a chance to show off her intellectual prowess.

'What does it mean?' Sue asked.

'No idea,' Maureen replied.

'I thought you spoke German,' Sue said.

'I do, but it's in French.'

'But don't you...,' but before Sue could finish, Maureen explained in exasperation, 'The letter is what you call crossed writing. So, it's a bit hard to decipher in places.'

'The writer's cross? What makes you think that?' Sue enquired. 'You really are good. Perhaps you should be a detective.'

'No, I mean it's crossed writing,' Maureen replied, her impatience growing by the minute. 'In the old days paper was expensive and when you sent a letter, you were charged for each sheet you included, you see, so people would try to use as few sheets as possible. Therefore, what people did, once they'd filled the page, they would turn the page so it was horizontal, in landscape as it were, and then write across what they had already written. So, you first need to read what is underneath, then turn the paper horizontally and read what's above.'

Maureen sensed, despite what she considered a detailed explanation, that Sue was none the wiser.

'How the hell do you know all that?' Sue gasped incredulously.

She was both impressed, despite not entirely understanding what Maureen had said, yet at the same time not fully convinced by Maureen's explanation. She had her doubts as to whether it was at all feasible to either write or read something like that. She had enough problems making out Maureen's writing on the various Post-it notes that Maureen would occasionally leave for her on the fridge door.

'Don't you remember?' Maureen explained, 'I used to work for the nuns at Tyburn typing up 19th century letters from and about their Foundress, Marie Adèle Garnier. I'm a bit of an expert when it comes to 19th century French crossed writing, even if I do say so myself.'

Here Maureen paused, unable to suppress a smug smile, so that both Walter and Sue could take in the enormity of that statement. She soon sensed she might be waiting some time so on second thoughts she decided to continue, 'I spent four years on and off typing those letters up. The irony is that I'm ace at reading crossed writing in French from the 19th century, but can't read my own handwriting.'

'You're not the only one,' Sue concurred.

'Can't you read this then?' Walter asked. 'I could see it was dated at the top Londres, janvier 1904 but couldn't make anything else out really.'

'Yes, I can make out most of it, if not all of it; the handwriting is awful in places but do you think this will help you track down the murderer?'

'I'm not sure but this was in the hand of his last victim so possibly? What does it say?'

'Weirdly it's about the convent. The gist is it's from some local priest to the Archbishop of Westminster. The priest is not happy that they've founded a convent in his parish. He's asking the Archbishop to close the convent down.'

'What's the name of the priest?' Sue asked.

'It looks as if it's,' Maureen hesitated, 'Charles Bingley.'

To be continued....

ABOUT THE AUTHOR

Maureen Younger is a comedian, writer, actor and polyglot, having previously lived in Austria, Russia, Ukraine, Spain, France and Germany. As a stand up comedian, she has performed throughout the UK and abroad and has occasionally performed stand up in both German and French. As an actor, roles range from appearing as an angry German housewife in Band of Brothers on TV to appearing in the play Roger and Miriam as Miriam, an alcoholic, Jewish, New Yorker with a gay son. She is also one third of the popular podcast, WTB alongside fellow comedians Jen Brister and Allyson June Smith. Maureen has also written articles for various magazines. For more information, please head to www.maureenyounger.com or on Twitter/Instagram/TikTok @maureenyounger.

.

Printed in Great Britain
by Amazon

23350211R00099